**She looked a**
**lived through**

Stockings ripped, legs covered in mud, skirt torn at its hem, hair mussed, nails chipped, wallet empty. Clay figured this ordinarily would have been a great personal tragedy for Jewell. But she just sat there with a bag of nacho chips—having already nearly cleaned out the vending machine on *his* dime—munching with ladylike daintiness.

There was only a shadow of vibrant color on her lips. Which was fine with Clay, because her lips looked a hell of a lot more kissable when they were natural.

He tried to concentrate on the week-old newspaper, and failed.

Clay didn't know if he thought Jewell was worthy of his anger, his contempt, his pity or his sexual hunger. All he knew was that this princess was in some kind of trouble.

## ABOUT THE AUTHOR

Most of Vivian Leiber's day involves carpools, peanut butter and jelly sandwich production, and laundry (lots of laundry). But there is a special part of every day in which she rediscovers the excitement and magic of romance. In the quiet time when she writes, she immerses herself in a different world and she invites the reader to join her. From her study, she has written stories that have made us laugh, made us cry, and have made us feel the electricity of the connection between a man and woman in love. Vivian lives in Illinois with her two sons, Joseph and Eastman, and her husband, Stephen.

## Books by Vivian Leiber

### HARLEQUIN AMERICAN ROMANCE
576—BABY MAKES NINE

# Vivian Leiber

## BLUE-JEANED PRINCE

# Harlequin Books

TORONTO • NEW YORK • LONDON
AMSTERDAM • PARIS • SYDNEY • HAMBURG
STOCKHOLM • ATHENS • TOKYO • MILAN
MADRID • WARSAW • BUDAPEST • AUCKLAND

This book is for Eastman and Joseph

ISBN 0-373-16640-0

BLUE-JEANED PRINCE

# Chapter One

Clay DeVries slowed his tow truck to a halt, considering only briefly that he might have trouble pulling out of the muddy troughs left by drivers before him. Leaning over the stick shift, he eased his head out of the passenger window, ignoring the sheets of rain and hail that came up every August afternoon from the Gulf of Mexico. His shirt, soaked with water and sweat and hard work, clung to his skin. Hard rain lashed his face, but still he stared.

He just couldn't believe what he saw.

She was a mirage, an oasis, the hallucinatory vision given to a man near to a bone-dry death in an isolated desert.

But he wasn't near death, the Mississippi Delta sure wasn't a desert and there was nothing, absolutely nothing, in a ten-mile radius that wasn't sopping wet.

Still, she was a mirage.

Because she sure couldn't be real.

Beauty like this didn't come to Clay DeVries.

Beauty like Jewell's.

Jewell Whittington.

Clay shook his head and ran his fingers through his ink black hair. He blinked several times, willing her away, willing her to stop tormenting him. But she remained—languidly dismissive of the storm, only grudgingly aware of him.

She leaned against the driver's-side door of a tomato red Fiat convertible, holding up a black umbrella to protect herself.

And she should be protected.

Protected. Coddled. Handled with care.

Clay knew she had had a lifetime of that.

A lifetime of protecting her fragile beauty from the likes of this storm, from the thick, oozing trail that passed for a road. A lifetime of protection from a man like him—a man who wasn't, and would never be, her equal.

He guessed her blond hair, the palest golden strands swept into a perfect twist, had been "done" that very afternoon. Her complexion—maybe the result of fancy makeup, maybe natural—was flawless, pale and luminous. Her lipstick, refined with a precise line of color, matched her fuchsia suit to a tee. The matching polished nails were perfectly manicured and ended in long, elegant ovals.

His eyes traveled the length of her, lingering when in any other circumstance he would have had no right to do more than glance in her direction from afar. Her eyes and her pursed lips commanded him to act like a gentleman, but since he had never been expected to be a gentleman in the past and had never enjoyed its benefits, he didn't see any reason to make the sacrifices of a gentleman now.

At least to look, he thought to himself.

And to smell the expensive perfume that mixed with the scent of rain.

He looked, letting his hooded eyes linger wherever he chose, as if she were spread before him on a magazine—he had never enjoyed that particular pleasure in any more than a fleeting way, but now, with Jewell Whittington passively before him, he understood the charms of a centerfold.

His gaze paused only as he felt his abdomen clench.

Those legs, he thought as he audibly gasped, went on for miles, beautiful miles.

And they ended at a pair of stiletto-heeled, black patent leather pumps that were sinking—slowly but surely—into the oozing mud of the ancient Native American trail leading to the Mississippi shoreline.

He looked up.

His eyes met hers. He thought he could study forever—get a degree even—in their pale color. Not quite blue. Not quite violet. Color that seemed to only deepen to shadow as her sooty lashes swept downward.

Her eyes narrowed as she coolly appraised him.

Dismissed him, too, with only the slightest fear— hidden well because she was a woman who was clearly shielded from men like him.

Men like him.

Brutes. Savages. Little better than animals.

Clay knew, with a twisting sensation in his gut, exactly what she saw, exactly what made her look away. He let his eyes drift only for a moment to the rearview mirror and saw for himself the grime, the sweat, the dirt. Mechanic's dirt. His T-shirt was soaked and torn slightly at the shoulders where a seam had burst while he strained to lift a customer's Chevy pickup from the ooze. His jeans, neatly pressed this morning—why, oh why did he even bother?—were caked with mud.

Clay reluctantly conceded to her disdain. He got out and stood in front of her, letting the driver's-side door hang open.

He felt nineteen again, working on the Whittington estate, assisting the gardener. Hard work. Sweaty work under a broiling Mississippi sun. And the best reward in those days wasn't the cash in the envelope given to him every Friday afternoon—that money went straight to his mother, to help raise his brothers and sisters.

No, the best payment for his work was when he'd catch sight of Jewell. In a smooth linen party dress. In a barely there bathing suit. In an evening gown as she waited for a suitor.

From far away, and always completely unobserved. For even when she saw him, her eyes would always pass right over him as if he were a willow tree or a wisteria shrub. He was invisible to her then because he was not her kind.

His admiration of her beauty had turned not so much sour as simply to indifference when he realized she would never see him.

But she was here now. And he was a man. Not a lovesick boy.

He knew the gossip.

Her suitors—so many from the very first cotillion given in the ballroom of her daddy's house—had married other pretty, suitable young ladies. And she, it was rumored, had been passed over. Again and again. And then she went to school, chasing more education and never finishing anything she started, all while what she really needed was a man.

Not a man like him, of course.

A dressed-up version, a cleansed version—with money.

That was her kind of man.

"Afternoon. Name's Clay DeVries," he said, wiping his hands with a handkerchief he kept in his back pocket.

"I ran out of gas," she said, her Southern drawl polite but impersonal. "Tow me back to the station, please."

Dropping her keys into his hand without any fleshly contact, she walked to the passenger's side of his truck, closed her umbrella and got inside.

He looked at the key chain.

Tiffany.

Sterling.

What else would a princess use? Certainly not the plastic key chain with a three-by-five-inch photo protected by polyurethane.

He decided, right then and there, he didn't like her any better for the passing of years. It was a feeling that emanated from his groin, swelled by her coolness and traveled throughout his body with the speed of electricity.

It wasn't that she held him in contempt, or even disliked him—somehow, Clay could have dealt with that. It wasn't that she feared him, as many sensible women might, here on an empty road, no witnesses, nowhere to run.

No, it was that she had completely dismissed him, as if he were of no more consequence than the tow truck itself.

He got in the cab of the truck, and maneuvered the tow into position. She closed her eyes, seemingly lost in sleep. But he knew it was simple evasion. She didn't want to talk to him.

*Fine,* he thought, *I've dealt with b—, ah, witches before.*

It took five minutes to get the red Fiat coupled to the truck, and he didn't bother to put the roof back up on it. Let her seat get soaked, for all he cared. He was soaked himself.

"All right, we're ready to go," he said when he got back in the cab.

She opened her eyes, and he felt contradictory pulses within him. He could almost envision the steno pad with a column of her good points on the right and bad points on the left.

On the left side—spoiled, glitzy, out of touch with real people, maybe even downright rude, conceited and not even willing to act like a decent human being to him.

On the right side—as beautiful as an angel, as delicately scented as a flower and maybe just as protected and innocent of the real world as a baby.

Though, of course, she had the tiniest lines at the corners of her eyes that showed her age, mid- to late twenties. Not quite his side of thirty. He couldn't remember whether she had been a year behind him in school—of course, she ran with a different crowd, so it would have been tough to know.

"Will you be taking me to Smith's station?"

"Yeah," he said.

"I hear he died this spring and there's going to be a new owner."

"That's right," he answered, and he waited for the next question.

*Who will be the new owner?*

The next logical question, one that he could have answered with his entire life story. And he wanted to tell it to her. All the hopes and dreams and ambitions. The hard work, the setbacks and the just plain persistence that might give him a shot at it. At Smith's station in the Natchez basin and at the three others. Profitable ones, money-makers, ready for expansion. He was going places; he was determined and ambitious. He had paid his dues, and now it was his turn to make himself the man he was meant to be.

But there wasn't a second question. She looked out at the cypress and pecan trees weighted down with Spanish moss, as if she were seeing them for the first time.

A princess regarding her subjects.

They didn't speak to each other as he drove through the softening storm. At the station, he uncoupled her car and filled it with gas. It was then that he noticed.

"When did you put gas in it last?" he asked, coming into the station's convenience store. She was leafing through a magazine. *Newsweek,* three years old. Clay realized how desperate she was to ignore him.

She blinked. "About two hours ago. I've been at school in Memphis and I'm comin' home. My daddy's taken sick again. Is something wrong with the car?"

"Your gas line is leaking. You need a new one. I can order it—for a Fiat it'll take a week or more for it to be delivered."

"A week! I can't do without my car for a week!"

"It's all right. I taped the line, it should do you till the part comes in. You can still drive it. At least a little, it'll get you home. But you need to bring it in when the part comes. I'll call."

"And you're sure you know how to work on Fiats?" she asked, narrowing her eyes at him.

He closed his eyes and began counting to ten.

"I'm just askin' because Smith couldn't handle anything foreign made. I usually got my car checked out in Memphis," she explained quickly. "I don't mean any harm by questioning. It's just that you're new, aren't you?"

He started over. *One, two, three, four...*

"I've been working for Smith for ten years," he said carefully. He left out that he had worked everywhere, taking any back-breaking job to raise his siblings and help support his mother, had even worked for the Whittingtons. But she didn't want to know all that.

"You aren't going to make it back to Memphis, even with the tape job. You need the line replaced before you leave."

"But I have to get back to Memphis!" she wailed. "I have a conference in three days! I'm giving a paper on Jane Austen. I can't possibly miss it!"

"What?"

Last he heard, she was getting a master's in some kind of history.

"Jane Austen," Jewell said primly, pronouncing each syllable carefully. "She was a very famous English writer of the nineteenth century."

"I know who Jane Austen is."

She just barely hid her surprise.

"Jane Austen, huh? What's it about?"

She settled her shoulders as if he had asked her a question she had been dying to answer. She could have no idea that Clay simply wanted to hear her talk, watch those flickering eyes, drink in her figure and perfume, maybe even glance a few times at her legs. The thirty-two-year-old Clay DeVries might think she was an airhead debutante with a bad attitude, but the nineteen-year-old still inside him thought she was worth an aching, nerve-tingling study.

"I'm writing about her life as a member of the privileged class."

"Uh-huh," Clay said. He wondered if her waist was tiny enough that he could span it with his own two hands.

Keep talking, he commanded her silently. He still wanted to look.

"So, for instance, she wrote a book called *Pride and Prejudice.*"

"I've read it," Clay said, thinking her breasts curved and strained at the fabric of her dress in just the right way to make a man forget all about anything except what was on the other side of her clothes.

The silence jolted him. He looked up at her face.

He was good at reading women. But Clay thought it was just that women liked having him around. No reading minds required.

But reading Jewell Whittington, he knew she was torn between wanting to slap him for his open appraisal of her physical charms and shock that he could read.

"I thought *Pride and Prejudice* was a nice story," Clay said with a wicked grin.

She was so pretty when she lost her footing, her picture-perfect confidence. He'd love it if she stayed off balance forever, if it meant she'd open up to him.

"Well, anyhow," she said, recovering quickly, "the book looks like an English country romantic comedy of manners, but my analysis shows that it's a withering documentary of oppression."

"Why don't you just enjoy the book?" Clay asked. "It was a book about some sisters finding their true loves."

"No, the book is really about oppression of women and the disappearance of the farming community in the face of the industrial revolution."

"Right."

She put her hands on her hips and squared off against him, angry more for his out-of-line looks than his ignorance of her field of study.

"I'm getting my master's degree in English literature, so I know what I'm talking about," she said. "And this paper is very important to me. My car has to be fixed, and I have to be at my conference in three days so I can present it. If you can't fix the car, you should tell me now."

"I'm as much of an expert in cars as you are in Jane Austen."

She almost, almost said something.

Suppressing a smile, Clay guessed that she would have conceded she wasn't the world's foremost expert on Austen.

Which left open the question of whether her precious car was in good hands.

"Well, I don't think we need to debate that point," she said smoothly. "Why don't you give me my keys? I'll take my chances on getting to Memphis with the tape on the gas line."

She held out her soft, pale hand with the five perfectly manicured nails.

That's when he noticed the rock.

Left hand.

Third finger.

Big.

Aggressively twinkling.

Off-limits.

He stared down at his own grimy hands. Strong hands. Callused hands. Worker's hands.

She was engaged.

He hid his shock, hid the part of him that had fantasized for a moment, hid his shame at having debased himself by dreaming of her without even having realized he had done so.

He wiped the keys with a Handi Wipe and gave them to her, forcing her to touch him. To acknowledge his flesh with her own. His fingers gripped the key chain for a second longer than was completely proper.

She looked away.

"Let's talk about you paying me," he said.

"What do you take?" she asked after only a moment's hesitation.

"What do you mean—take?"

"What credit card?"

"We don't do credit cards. Smith never had credit cards on-line."

She pulled a sleek alligator wallet from her black linen purse and rifled through it.

"I've got three dollars."

"That's not enough."

Her chin tilted defiantly.

"Then what am I supposed to do?"

He stared at her. Hard.

Now that the fantasy had been destroyed, now that he knew she belonged to another man, he didn't care what she thought of him.

She stepped back, eyes widened.

It took him a second to realize what she was thinking.

Clay was his own version of a gentleman, even if he had grown up on the wrong side of the tracks. He would never demand the kind of payment she was thinking of. But how he enjoyed the shock on her face. He reveled in the moment, only briefly, when she considered the kind of pleasure she would get from him, the kind of pleasure she would have to return. The violet of her eyes sparkled as she stared. And then she bit her lower lip.

"I'm engaged, you know," she said, twisting nervously at the marble-size diamond. "To Winfield Sims. The fourth."

"Best wishes," Clay said blandly, remembering that men were to be congratulated on their engagements, women to be wished all the best. Men were presumed to have concluded a successful courtship, women to have been caught. Looking at her, Clay had to admit that Winfield deserved some congratulations—and a smidgen of envy. "All this is irrelevant to how you're going to pay."

"My father will send you a check," she said brusquely. "Charles Whittington. We're the Whittingtons of the Pontchartreaux estate."

"I know exactly who you are, Jewell."

She paused only a moment, surprised at his use of her first name.

And then she turned on her heel and strode out the door with her head held high.

Each night for the next three weeks, Clay awoke from the same dream. Jewell Whittington was beneath him, moaning with pleasure, her hair damp and loosened from its pins. He had thought he had gotten over her—many years ago.

"AND WHILE I LOVE JEWELL, I feel it is in her best interests for her to develop independence, self-discipline, initiative and self-reliance. In the event, of course, that she does not marry. Therefore, I leave to my beloved daughter nothing of material value but my boundless love, which will remain true forever."

"What do you mean, nothing?" Jewell asked.

Thomas Fogerty III rustled the papers before him and adjusted his glasses. He closed his eyes and tried once more to read the shocking paragraph.

"And while I love Jewell, I feel—"

"No, I heard you the first time. I mean, explain it to me. The nothing part."

"By the terms of this most recently executed will, your father has left everything to Milwaukee's New

Hope homeless shelter run by his son, your half brother, Michael." Thomas nodded quickly at Michael Whittington, who sat in solemn quiet on the armchair by the unused fireplace. "Jewell, sweetie, you are not left anything. Except, of course, for your personal effects."

Thomas placed the papers before him on the mahogany desk. He looked at Jewell. She seemed puzzled. Or stunned. As if somebody had knocked her over the head.

"Jewell, if you're marrying Winfield, you don't need his money anyhow," Thomas said.

"And if I'm not?"

Thomas coughed and took a quick sip of sherry from the glass in front of him. Crystal. With a rolling-script *W* engraved on the side.

"If you don't get married, your father hopes you'll learn some of these fine personal attributes."

"By not having any money?"

Thomas looked down at his papers.

His eyes skirted over to Michael Whittington, who was leaning back in the velvet chair as if he were engaged in a private, silent but highly personal conversation with the Lord. Only thirty-four years old and already he was showing the effects of years of personal abuse.

Only moments before, Michael had explained that the wild life was all behind him—he had even become a servant to the very people he had once exploited. The homeless, the addicted, the fringe of society—really quite a noble and inspiring story. Thomas looked again at Jewell. Maybe this was for the best. Build some character, escape the curse of bloated living that befell the wealthy scions of Pontchartreaux.

"I thought Daddy was going to leave me everything he owned. I just assumed..."

A discreet cough from Rev. James Copland caught Jewell's attention.

"With a generous gift to our church, of course," she added, nodding at the man who had been the family spiritual guide, or at least the Sunday dinner guest, for the past twenty years.

"Well, all that's been changed," Michael said, rising to his feet. "Father felt strongly about my turnaround. I've worked hard in the past three years to give back to the community that saved my life from the gutter. New Hope gives exactly what its name suggests—new hope to those in need."

"I think your work sounds very important," Rev. Copland said, sounding surprisingly good-natured, considering that he had just witnessed millions of dollars slipping out of his own church's grasp.

"It is important," Michael agreed. "I've raised a lot of hell in my life—pardon my blunt language, but it's true. I've been an embarrassment to my father, no question about it. But I've changed. And New Hope helps me as much as it does those who come to our doors every day. Father was very proud of my work. And I know he wanted to see us succeed. The money he has left us will mean so much."

"If he was so impressed, why didn't he invite you for Christmas or Thanksgiving dinner?" Jewell asked. Her half brother's name hadn't even been mentioned in the house for years, and she was shocked—even a little suspicious—of this new Michael.

"I would have loved to come," Michael said with a wistful smile. "But those holidays are ones where the homeless have the most need. I couldn't abandon them at a time when all society turns its back on those most degraded by life's hardships."

Thomas coughed. "I know it's a shock, Jewell," he said. "But you can't fault your father for wanting to fund something like this. Sounds like Michael does some very good things for people, and your father always wanted to do right by others. He was a generous man and he must have thought that you didn't need any more money. You and Winfield will have plenty."

Jewell bit her lip. "Are you suggesting that I distrust Michael because I'm greedy?"

Thomas looked away.

"I just don't understand it," Jewell said.

"Father probably would have explained how we were becoming closer," Michael said gently. "But you've been so busy...with school. Actually, school was one of the reasons that Father thought you should be out on your own. Making your own way."

That stopped Jewell in her tracks. She settled into the cushions of the couch quietly and raised not a protest as Thomas completed reading the final technical details of the will.

School.

That had definitely been a point of controversy between her and her father—had he decided that, at twenty-eight, she needed to finally get out of the ivory tower and into the real world?

Or at least make up her mind what she wanted to be when she grew up.

But she needed just a few more months to finish her master's in literature. And her diploma would hang upstairs—next to the master's in American economic history from SMU and the bachelor's in sociology from Texas A&M. And, like ghosts, there were the programs she had started with enthusiasm and dropped out of when they proved unfulfilling—the Cordon Bleu Cooking Institute, the Parson's School of Design, the Art Institute of Chicago. No degrees, but memories and a smattering of skills.

In a few months, she'd have that master's.

Then, armed with all this education, she would do...something.

"So what now?" Jewell asked as Thomas folded the will and placed it inside a manila folder.

Thomas looked at Michael, and something unreadable passed between the two men.

"Please, Jewell, it is a shock," Thomas said at last. "But I see many people whose parents have left them money, and often it's not for the good."

"It's not the money."

"I'm sure you're right," he said, sounding unconvinced.

"It's not. I just don't understand why my father would leave me with nothing."

"The will explains itself," Thomas said testily. "Jewell, I think you have to come to grips with the fact that you and Winfield will have to live on the money the Simses have. What's so bad about that? He is, after all, extremely wealthy in his own right. A few million here or there isn't going to make a difference."

"I want what is mine," Jewell said, staring intently at her half brother. She hadn't met Michael more than two or three times in her life, but she knew now she didn't like him.

"You've always been so ladylike," Thomas said quietly. "It was—is—your finest quality."

His words seemed to echo through the study. Rev. Copland looked about uncomfortably. Michael stared at the fireplace. Thomas riffled absently through the papers before him. The grandfather clock in the front hallway announced five o'clock. Martha's footsteps could be heard upstairs as she readied the house for evening.

"What happens to me?" Jewell asked. "I mean, if Winfield doesn't marry me? Or if I decide I don't want to marry Winfield?"

"Either way, you don't have any Whittington money," Michael said coolly.

"So what am I supposed to do?"

"Set a wedding date," Michael urged.

Jewell stared at her half brother.

"I'm sure Michael would provide for you," Thomas said. He took out a finely gauged cotton handkerchief and mopped the beads of sweat that had popped up on his forehead. "Wouldn't you, Michael?"

Charles's divorce from Michael's mother nearly thirty-one years before had been ugly and contentious. Now Thomas wondered if Charles should have been a little gentler, a little more generous with his first wife. Maybe Michael wouldn't have turned out the way he had if Charles had been more careful....

"Of course Michael will care for his sister," Rev. Copland said confidently.

Michael stood up and strolled to the window over-looking the sweeping garden of azalea and rose—the flowers drooped from days of rain.

Jewell twisted nervously at the ring on her left hand.

She wondered how Winfield would react to the news that her father had left everything to Michael.

It wouldn't change things, would it? she wondered, staring out the window past Michael. She had been engaged to Winfield for two years now and she had nearly forgotten that engagement was connected with marriage. The days when she leafed through *Southern Bride* magazine and debated what color her brides-maids should wear were long over.

Marry Winfield?

Oh, yeah, that's what the ring on her finger was all about.

"I would be happy for Jewell to come work at the New Hope with me if her wedding to Winfield doesn't come off," Michael said at last. "But I know Father thought very highly of Winfield. I've never met Win-field myself, but Father told me many times that he was great for Jewell."

At last, this was something everyone in the room could agree upon. Thomas, Rev. Copland and Jewell nodded, thinking of how Winfield had been so close to Charles.

"How he wished that he could have lived long enough to witness his daughter's wedding," Michael continued.

Again, nods.

And for Jewell, a small, niggling guilt that she hadn't moved a little more quickly. Gotten married, given her father a grandchild... She did miss him in spite of everything.

"So I hope the couple will move with all speed toward a wedding," Michael said. "I would be so happy to give the bride away."

While Jewell put her head in her hands, she noticed Thomas's head bobbing like a buoy in water. Rev. Copland was content to express his agreement by a thin, wavering smile.

The thought of going down the aisle on Michael's arm was strangely disturbing.

"What if we don't get married?" Jewell asked. "That's my birthright we're talking about."

Michael's face briefly flushed at the word *birthright*. Jewell gasped and nearly apologized. Her father had, after all, virtually abandoned his first family in all but the financial sense. She could see that Michael might be sensitive to the fact that he had never been treated as a son to Charles—although she, like her father, would have said it was Michael's own fault.

But maybe his nefarious experiences were precisely what was necessary to create a caring servant of the poor.

"I think we should remember, as harsh as it sounds, that my father was very determined that the New Hope homeless shelter should be fully funded," Michael said. "After all, he had always known the security of the family home—even in times of financial hardship. He wanted others to have the same chances he did. Each dollar that I were to spend maintaining Jewell's life-style in the manner she's accustomed to would be money taken from the hands of the needy. I'm sure that Jewell isn't so selfish..."

He let his words hang in the air as each man studied Jewell. She suddenly felt self-conscious about the understated but overpriced black bouclé Chanel suit that had been just right for the funeral. The matching Ferragamo pumps. The Hermes scarf at her shoulder. She didn't own many pieces of "important" jewelry—and certainly hadn't worn anything to the funeral—except for her engagement ring, which suddenly seemed far larger than the four carats Winfield had claimed it was.

"Of course I'm not against feeding and sheltering the homeless," she said hesitantly. "And I would never want to go against my father's wishes. I apologize—I was taken by surprise."

"So were we all," said Rev. Copland dryly.

JEWELL TURNED THE KEY in the ignition once more.

Nothing.

Nothing but cicadas and the sweep of the willow trees and the growling of her stomach. She was hungry. Very hungry. The only thing she had eaten since the funeral was a half-melted Snickers bar she had found in her purse.

The call to Winfield was a disaster. Nice, friendly, but still—goodbye. Winfield's family—gossip sure traveled fast on the delta—was adamant that Winfield break things off.

Wimp, Jewell had thought to herself as they hung up. She wasn't sure she really wanted to marry him anyhow, but it was pretty despicable that he couldn't even stand up to his family on matters of the heart.

Michael's reaction to the breakup of her engagement had been very curious. He was enraged. He was

shocked. He accused her of sabotaging a relationship. He demanded she call back Winfield and beg him
to take her back. Which only made her pride rear up,
and so she had refused.

"You have two choices, Jewell," he had shrieked.
"You can get your butt up to Milwaukee where you'll
volunteer at my shelter or you clear out of here and I
don't ever want to see you again."

"I wouldn't work at your shelter if you paid me,"
Jewell cried out indignantly. "I don't buy your born-
again-human malarkey. And I know you're up to
some scam. Furthermore, I think it's despicable that
you are taking advantage of the less fortunate for
your—"

"I knew it," Michael said, pouncing on her words.
"You're selfish and don't want to help others. You've
been spoiled. You don't understand what it means to
struggle every day like the average person."

Twenty minutes later, amid fierce yelling and a few
choice words that Jewell hadn't suspected she had
known—much less ever used—she was on the street.

"It's your choice to leave!" Michael shrieked.
"Don't go blaming me for this—I would have been
happy to have you work for me, I would have been
happy to give you a nice wedding, but no..."

Thinking back to his words, she shook her head and
then rested it on the steering wheel. The gas line. The
guy had said something about a gas line. For a moment, her thoughts drifted—call it a hallucination
brought on by stress and hunger, shock and thirst—
but she swore she could remember every detail of him.

Except his name.

But his name wasn't important.

She thought of his broad shoulders, his blatantly sexual stance, his raven-colored hair and his brown eyes.

Great.

*Jewell Whittington, you're having the worst day of your entire life and you're thinking about a mechanic you met three weeks ago?*

As she always did when she was nervous, she pulled the battery-lit, sterling silver, engraved makeup mirror from her glove compartment. Checking her hair, she hesitantly pulled several bobby pins that had come askew. Then she yanked an errant lock and tried to pin it back into place. But it didn't look quite right. She pinned and coaxed and pulled and teased.

Nothing worked.

Suddenly, she burst into tears, letting the mirror fall to the floor of her car.

She had held back her tears when the nurse had called her at school to tell her that Daddy had been rushed to the hospital with chest pains. She had held back her tears when she had made her final goodbyes in the intensive-care unit. She hadn't wept at all at the funeral, maintaining a quietly regal poise as hundreds of mourners pressed her hand. She hadn't even shed a tear at the reading of the will, and certainly not a whimper at the break up of her engagement or the screaming match with Michael in the front courtyard of Pontchartreaux.

But now she cried, and it was for all the wrong reasons, she knew.

She wasn't crying for her father; she was crying for herself. She felt selfish and angry at herself for being selfish. For feeling so lost. Maybe she was spoiled.

Maybe she didn't help others enough, although the prospect of working with her half brother at any enterprise was too upsetting to contemplate.

But she wasn't that bad, was she?

Why, she had attended countless charity dinners and had even chaired the annual Cancer Society Ball three times!

And she always helped out her friends as best she could.

And she had only left her sociology studies because, in the end, she didn't feel that she was very good at it—or maybe it was because, even armed with a degree, she felt a yawning emptiness inside of her.

She looked into the mirror and saw a disgusting mess.

How could he have raised her like this, unable to even do her own hair—and then have cut her loose so abruptly?

He had raised her alone, Jewell's mother having died when Jewell was just two. He had raised her to be ornamental, to be cared for by others—and he had paid a fortune to those who had done the work. Nannies, riding trainers, drivers, hairdressers, dance instructors. She was almost thirty and had never had a job, didn't have the slightest clue as to how to get one. She had watched the waitresses at the club once and marveled at how they kept everybody's orders straight. She had decided that the skills necessary to be a waitress were beyond her. And her father had agreed, laughing.

Driving the Fiat by herself and going to college were the only two things she had managed on her own.

She knew how to go to college better than anybody. In fact, she did it so well she had a terrible time every spring that a graduation loomed. But a talk with her father had always resulted in an assurance that another degree, work in a related field of study or even striking out in a new academic direction was just the thing she needed. So she had stayed in school, occasionally worrying that she would become a perpetual student. One of those that couldn't finish up their thesis after five, ten, fifteen years.

Well, one less worry. Because her father hadn't even paid the tuition bill for the semester she was finishing up now. And Michael wasn't likely to spring for the bill.

End of perpetual-studenthood worries.

Now she needed to find a place to stay for the night. Or at least dinner.

She stopped herself from thinking as far into the future as the next day because it was just too painful.

She dried her tears with a mascara-preserving swipe and then pulled out the bobby pin she had just put in.

And then she pulled another and another. In minutes, she destroyed the French twist that had taken the hairdresser who had come to the house that morning forty-five minutes to arrange. Jewell brusquely pulled a comb through her hair, wincing as she worked through tangles, missed pins and hardened hair spray.

Her hair finished—though not good enough for an evening on the town—she opened the car door.

This'll be the first step to a new life, she thought with forced and vague optimism. I'll get a job, my own place, make a life for myself. Father would be so proud.

She stood on her Prada pumps and took her purse and her cosmetic case. The cosmetics case contained her small collection of jewelry—a few bracelets and necklaces, which she knew she would have to sell—and since it was far too heavy to carry, she locked it, with her suitcase of clothes, in the Fiat's trunk.

Now, a gas station.

An hour and a half later, she walked barefoot because one of the heels on her shoes had split from its sole. She was thirsty, she needed to pee, she had been frightened off the road by a group of rowdy teen boys shouting from their cars and she wanted very desperately to put her head down somewhere and sleep.

She felt the headlights behind her, and she started to veer to the side of the road. But mud oozed through the spaces between her toes, and she thought she would go mad at the outraged whine of bullfrogs. Were there snakes around here? She wondered if water moccasins came up with the rain-swollen river. And what about gators?

She turned around just as the truck pulled to her side. She looked into the cab and didn't know if she felt elation, relief or depression as she saw the driver.

They stared at each other for nearly a minute. He seemed puzzled. She wondered if she should run.

"Did I remember to pay you?" she asked hopefully.

"No," he said sourly, sliding over to shove open the passenger's-side door. "I'd have been terribly surprised if you had."

## Chapter Two

The princess didn't look too good, Clay thought, so he didn't ask any questions on the road. When he unlocked the station, he sat down on the stool by the cash register, rested his elbows on the counter and his head in his hands and watched her eat. All without saying a single word.

A bag of nacho chips.

Two bags of Cheez-Its.

Four Slim Jims.

Two Hostess Twinkies.

A bag of Skittles.

Washed down with two twenty-ounce bottles of Dr. Pepper.

She didn't look at him once while she was engaging in this massive pig-out. She made her selections one at a time and then sat on the fold-out chair by the window to consume them with ladylike daintiness. She had something on her mind, some worry or obsession that took up every thought.

Probably about how *The Cat in the Hat* was really about the oppression of mice, Clay figured.

He could have been kidnapped by aliens or turned into a pumpkin, and she'd never notice. She never once acknowledged his presence. She craned her neck when she noticed the Pretty Good Café across the street, but the café had been closed for years. As hungry as she was, she probably could have single-handedly brought the business back to life.

Clay studied her, all the while pretending to read the *National Enquirer* spread out on the counter in front of him.

As if she cared what he did.

What she should be caring about was that she looked as if she had lived through a tornado.

Her stockings were ripped to shreds, her feet and legs covered with mud, scratches and bug bites. Her black skirt had a rip at its hem. Her hair went in all different directions. Her nails were chipped—Clay figured this ordinarily would have been a great personal tragedy. And her lips had only a shadow of her signature vibrant fuchsia color.

Which was fine with Clay, because her lips looked a hell of a lot more kissable when they were natural.

Now, where had that thought come from? he wondered.

He tried to concentrate on the article about the alien quintuplets born in California.

Clay didn't know if he thought she was worthy of his anger, his contempt, his pity or his sexual hunger. All he knew was that this princess was in some kind of trouble.

The same higher power that put this undeniably beautiful woman in Clay's path apparently expected him to help her out of a jam.

Stray dogs. Cats with a big litter and no Meow Mix. Moms with fifty cents in their pocket, no milk in the fridge and six days to payday. Kids with popped bicycle tires, empty pockets and a wide-eyed look as they stared into the freezer filled with ice-cream sandwiches and Popsicles.

Clay was the last resort of many, and it shouldn't have come as any surprise to him that Jewell would end up in his care.

Crumpling up the Twinkies cellophane and popping it into the wastebasket, she discreetly burped behind her hand. Then, and only then, did she honor him with her attention.

"Let's go," she said.

"What do you mean, let's go?"

"Let's go get my car."

"Look, Princess, it's ten-thirty at night. I'm not going anywhere."

"The gas station is closed, right?" she asked, pointing to the Closed sign that he had placed in the corner window when they had entered. "That means you don't have to stay here guarding the cash register. So let's go. You can tow my car back here to the station and fix the gas line you were complaining about last time."

He shook his head. The day had been too long for this kind of aggravation.

"We're not going anywhere."

"I can't leave my car out there overnight! Somebody might steal it!"

Clay shrugged. "So it gets stolen. Have your daddy buy another one."

The look on her face made Clay regret that last comment.

An emotion, fleeting and harrowing, cracked the surface of her poise.

But only for a moment. She might have lost a lot of things tonight—and Clay could only guess what—but her sense of privilege wasn't something she had forfeited.

"Is this because I forgot to pay you for the last time? Because if it is, I can pay up now. Visa or American Express?"

"No, no credit cards," he said.

"Whoever buys this place should start using credit cards. Everybody does. I never carry cash."

"I've noticed."

"And you should have healthier snacks for people to buy."

"You didn't seem to mind what we had."

"Only because there wasn't anything else. Maybe you should bring this up with the new owner. Better yet, maybe you should buy the place," she fired back. "Then you can eliminate money and put in credit cards and stock the shelves with something decent to eat, maybe rice cakes and certainly Evian or Perrier."

"Yeah, right. Me. Owning the place."

"I was just joking. How could a mechanic scrape up the money...?"

She realized she was looking straight into the unforgiving eyes of a bona fide, honest-to-God mechanic.

"Sorry. That came out wrong."

"I understand."

"It's been a terrible day."

"Princess, why don't you pay up and get on your way?" Clay asked gently.

"Stop calling me Princess. I'm not one," she said. "Anymore."

Clay looked more closely at her. She had definitely gone through some terrible trial. What kind, he could only guess.

"I'll see if I've got cash," she said.

She rifled through her purse and pulled out a luxuriously soft ostrich wallet. She pulled out three worn bills and augmented them with a few coins.

"There," she said proudly as she shoved the money toward him. The coins made a tinny sound as they hit the counter. "Sixteen dollars and forty-three cents. Let's go get my car."

"Keep it. That barely covers what you just ate for dinner," he said. "Besides, I really don't like to take the tow out this late, and all the money you have isn't going to change my mind."

She looked as if she might burst into tears, and Clay felt like a coward.

"Here—this'll pay you," she said. "This is worth a hell of a lot of money. And I've never met a man who wasn't moved by money."

He was startled at her use of profanity.

"Take it," she commanded.

He looked down at the diamond solitaire.

"You forget that we've been down this road before. And you didn't offer me diamonds the last time. What happened to your fiancé?"

She shook her head. "Don't ask, just take it."

He closed his eyes and wondered when was the last night he had gotten a decent sleep. The station had to be open at six, and he still had to do the evening's books for the three other stations scattered around the Natchez. Sometimes, he wondered if he had taken on more than he could handle, but his ambition and his raw determination to succeed pushed him. Had always pushed him.

Pushed him to the very limits of his endurance and strength. Pushed him so hard that now, as his goal seemed so in reach, he felt only exhaustion. And the emptiness of wondering what it was all for.

He hadn't had that problem when he was a teen and had a family to support. But now, lurking in his heart was the why of it all.

"It's so important to you to get the car tonight?" he asked defeatedly.

"Yes. Everything I—"

She stopped herself. But Clay could finish the sentence for her without any trouble. He could see it in her eyes, the way they skittered back and forth, terrified of the uncertainty more than any particular deprivation.

Somehow, she had lost everything.

Jewell Whittington was no better off than the average, middle-of-the-road, trying-to-make-a-living person.

Worse, Clay guessed from the looks of things. He wondered why he didn't feel any satisfaction from knowing that.

There had been a time when he would have been delighted at witnessing her downfall, had even daydreamed of a shamed and humiliated Jewell who would have no other option but to plead with him for help. There was no other way that he could imagine her coming to him, no other way that he could have conjured up a vision of her bending to him.

But that time was long ago—he had been just a boy, still in high school, uncertain of his own strengths and easily embarrassed by the persistent grass stains on his jeans or the worn, dusty color of his shirts, easily shamed by his poverty and lack of social grace. That Jewell Whittington was beyond his grasp had seemed an epic tragedy.

Now he was a man. Certain of his prowess, comfortable with his abilities, proud of his accomplishments, sure of his future—or, at least, sure that he would overcome anything, everything that held him down. And he knew enough of the real tragedies of life to understand that whether Jewell Whittington was within his reach because of a momentary change of her fortunes was interesting but not earth-shattering.

In fact, if anything, he would say he no longer "fancied" her. Jewell, she was too fragile. Too delicate. Raised as a pampered house cat. He liked his women strong and understanding and warm—although he confessed to a weak spot for leggy blondes.

Which brought him right back to Jewell.

Best to get her on her way.

And quick about it.

"Okay, you win," he said. "Let's go."

He jumped over the counter and, as he reached the door, she touched his arm.

She pointed to her diamond ring on the counter. Clay shook his head.

"Save it," he said. "You'll need it more than I do. Wherever you're going. Whatever it is you're going to do."

FOR THE SECOND TIME in three weeks, Clay coupled the red Fiat to the back of the tow truck. This time was a little trickier than the last.

The Fiat was trashed.

The front tires had been punctured.

The hood ornament had been ripped from its screws.

The windshield wipers had been bent out of shape.

There was other damage to the car, and Clay figured it was kids out looking for trouble instead of professionals who had had their fun on the tiny sports car.

But Jewell's suitcase and cosmetics case had been stolen from the trunk.

She didn't say a word when they saw the open, empty trunk.

Just took a deep breath and walked over to the passenger's side of the tow truck and waited inside for him.

"It's all right, Jewell," he said as he slid into the driver's side. "It's just things. Things can always be replaced."

She shook her head, her blond hair falling toward her face. In the dark, he couldn't see—but he heard a sudden choking and he knew she was crying.

"Everything I owned was in that suitcase!" she wailed. "And the cosmetics case had all my jewelry."

"You can replace that stuff," he said. "Trust me, I've been there. With nothing but the shirt on my back. And look at me now."

She pushed her hair away from her tearstained face and regarded him carefully. Clay realized that, to her eyes, he was nothing more than a mechanic, a gas-station attendant, somebody who filled the tank and checked the oil. Nothing but a car jockey. *Look at me now* weren't very reassuring words to her.

"I can't buy new of anything," she explained peevishly. Taking a deep breath, she exhaled shakily. "My father died, leaving me nothing. And my half brother and I had a big fight and I ended up leaving. Or maybe thrown out—there's not much difference. I don't have a penny to my name, I don't have a place to live, I've lost everything."

"So you'll have to get a job," Clay said, feeling contradictory emotions of empathy and irritation.

"Just like that? Get a job?"

"What do you know how to do?"

"Nothing! Absolutely nothing. I mean, I know how to throw a dinner for fifty close friends and I know which wines to serve to them. I can tell the difference between Manet and Monet. And I can tell you the life stories of twenty-five overlooked women writers of the last century. But there aren't many teaching jobs available unless you have a Ph.D., nobody needs a hostess and I can't take dictation, or run a cash register. What kind of job can I get?"

"You could probably do some serious damage on 'Jeopardy,'" Clay said.

She nearly laughed, but then shook her head dismally. Clay thought he saw the first glimmerings of wet tears on her cheeks.

"Oh, Jewell, I'm sorry about all this."

He reached out to her and pulled her into his embrace. He breathed in the intoxicating mixture of perfume and talc that emanated from her. He meant his contact as comforting, but as he closed his eyes and settled her body next to his, he felt a rebellious stirring in his groin.

Her trembling stopped. Her breath stilled. And her back stiffened. She looked up at him, her breath a reluctant caress in the hot, humid darkness.

Their eyes met. Hers glittering in subdued reflection of the headlights of his truck. His eyes dark as oil and as hard as steel—but not without the hot-as-flame desire, never quenched during youth and now, even with all his hard-won maturity, reignited by their brief embrace.

She pulled away from him and slid to the farthest reaches of the seat.

He turned the key on the ignition and sighed.

"Sorry," he said. "Didn't mean anything. Just wanted to say I'm sorry you're in so much trouble."

"No problem," she said, dismissing him curtly.

He pulled the truck out onto the highway and into the night.

It would have meant more to him to hear outrage, to feel her anger at his presumption slap against his face as sternly as her palm.


"I DON'T THINK we should go in," he said, staring up at the front door of L'Hermitage, the finest restaurant in the Natchez valley. "You don't know if your credit card will work."

"I hardly think Michael could cancel my American Express," Jewell replied tartly. "Come on. You want to get paid, don't you? Your station doesn't take credit cards, and I don't have cash. So this is the only way I can express my appreciation."

Clay shrugged. Actually, he'd just like to go home and get into bed. But she was very determined to treat him to dinner, and Clay felt himself drawn to obey her invitation. If only to make her feel better.

"Come on, Clay, let me treat you. What other way do I have of showing you how grateful I am?"

A gentleman wouldn't tell her the myriad ways he could think of for her to pay him back for the tow. She could start with a lingering kiss and by putting one of those perfectly manicured hands on his clenched stomach. Just for starters.

He'd say that to another woman.

But something stopped him from saying that to her.

As they pulled into the nearly empty parking lot, Clay realized it was almost midnight.

"Are you sure you want to do this?" he asked, thinking that a Dixie longneck and a plate of fried catfish at his brother Al's roadhouse would be a hell of a lot better and a hell of a lot less hassle.

"No, really, you've been very nice to me," Jewell said, misinterpreting his question and assuming that he was simply shy about accepting such a generous treat.

She checked her compact, fixed her makeup as best she could, slipped out of her shredded stockings—the bare legs, though scratched and muddied, looked better—and ripped the lone heel from its sole so that she created matching flats from her stiletto-heeled pumps.

She regarded Clay, in his plain white T-shirt and faded jeans. He wasn't dirty or grimy as he had been the first time they had met—and she couldn't cast stones when her own appearance left something to be desired.

But still...

"I'll ask Henri to give you a suit jacket," she said, smiling apologetically. "They require men to wear jackets and ties, but the maître d' can usually scare up a jacket for someone who has forgotten his."

She spritzed a little Chanel No 5 on her wrists and at the back of her ears from a small atomizer she kept in her purse. Her confidence was returning, and Clay knew what a triumph it was for her to even get this far. She had spunk, and more courage than she herself even realized. More than anyone else would give her credit for.

He recognized a little of himself in her—a little of the reckless determination of his youth.

Maybe it would do her good to go into L'Hermitage, and with that, he set aside his misgivings.

She wordlessly handed him a delicate tortoiseshell comb from her purse.

Frowning, he took it.

Just when he was starting to warm to her, she invariably did something that would remind him that she thought of him as her inferior. Which he was. Until tonight.

*We're all equal here, Princess,* he thought sardonically.

But he didn't have the heart to point that out to her.

He combed his dark hair. Even he had to admit he had needed it. His appearance, other than a good scrubbing at the end of the day, never entered his consciousness. Women had always taken him exactly as he came. No complaints until this evening.

"Come on," she ordered lightly.

He followed her across the gravel lot to the white Greek Revival mansion with its ornate Corinthian columns lining the wraparound porch. A doorman bowed and pulled the gold door handle, which was cast in the shape of an arching fish. Inside, lush palms and oversize wicker furniture adorned the giant entranceway.

"M'selle Whittington!" a French-accented voice trilled. "A pleasure to see you once more."

A diminutive man in a white dinner jacket appeared out of nowhere to kiss Jewell's hand and exclaim mightily about his bottomless grief that she had not been to dinner here more frequently. If he had anything to say about her torn dress, her uncoiffed hair, her mud-splattered legs—he didn't mention it.

"Henri, give us a table, kind of out-of-the-way," Jewell said. She stepped back to show him Clay. "This gentleman needs a jacket. I'll be in the ladies' room freshening up."

Henri led Clay to a closet beneath the grand staircase. He handed him a blue sport coat.

"M'selle Whittington is the fiancée of Winfield Sims IV," Henri said with casual French arrogance. "And I think you are completely out of your league, if you don't mind my saying so."

"I'm not out of my league. Not tonight, buddy."

"Is she yours?"

"Such an indiscreet question, Henri," Clay replied with just enough bite so that the diminutive maître d' knew he was serious. "But the answer is no. She's not mine."

"I wouldn't think so," Henri said, and then he dropped his fancy accent for a low-down Southern drawl. "M'selle Whittington is used to the finer things."

"Listen, she's just taking me to dinner."

"Well, good luck."

Clay slipped on the jacket.

"Ah, and here is the beauty!" Henri cried out, French persona firmly in place once more. "M'selle Whittington, I have found the perfect table for you and your, uh, guest."

Clay smiled. Henri had put the perfect, subdued intonation of disapproval on the word *guest*.

Clay suddenly realized that Jewell must feel quite daring bringing the likes of Clay DeVries to L'Hermitage. He felt used, but still, he followed Henri and Jewell to their "out-of-the-way" table on the outside patio.

She might be using him, but he had never been inside this place—and he hated himself for the truth that he was thrilled to get a chance to peek at how the other half lived. The other half that would one day be his, if he worked hard.

He noticed that her legs were now clean—smooth and creamy colored—and still as long as forever. Even in the flats, she was a tall, striking woman. Heads turned as they passed through the main dining room. He didn't notice that women gave him their appraisal as much as the men did to Jewell.

The patio was surrounded by a wall of hibiscus, and beyond the magnolia trees, they could see the twinkling lights of two casino boats slowly drifting down the Mississippi River.

"This will do, *m'selle?*" Henri asked as he helped Jewell into her seat and handed menus to both of them.

"This will do," Jewell said in a voice that faltered between regalness and uncertainty in her new position as a dethroned princess.

"WHAT AM I DOING WRONG?"

Jewell was startled. "Sorry?" she asked.

"I asked you what I was doing wrong."

"Nothing," she said absently, suddenly aware that she had let her mind wander to her own problems when she should, as hostess, be more attentive to Clay.

"I'm using the wrong fork. Is that it?"

She looked at his place setting and at the fork in his hand. As recently as yesterday, the sight of a man using his fish fork to eat salad would have shocked and appalled her.

"Clay, you have the right to use whatever fork you want to," she said with perfect Southern warmth. She picked up her fish fork and held it aloft over her untouched salad.

His eyes narrowed. "No, don't patronize me. If I was an investment banker from up north, you would tell me the truth. I want to know," he insisted. "You're just using the same fork now to make me feel comfortable."

Jewell opened her mouth to protest, and then realized he was absolutely right—on both counts.

"If you're determined to learn, you use the outermost fork first," she said, pointing to his salad fork.

"Thank you," Clay said, putting back the fish fork and picking up the right one.

Jewell regretted her sharp tone with him. He was the only person who had been nice to her in the past two days. Her father had left her penniless. Michael had been a jerk, even if he was supposedly a saint to the common man. Winfield had broke up with her because he couldn't stand up to his family. And just now, in the ladies' room, a half-dozen phone calls to her "closest" friends had revealed two important truths.

Everyone in the delta knew she didn't have a dime.

And nobody in the delta had a spare bedroom for her.

She tried not to think about the possibility that she had lost her friends with her money.

"I should be thanking you for all you've done today," Jewell said. She put on her best hostess smile. "Clay, why don't you tell me a little about yourself? Where did you grow up?"

Perfect opener, she thought with something approaching smugness. Everyone liked to talk about themselves, and how often had she played a gracious hostess with that opening line?

"I grew up right here," he said curtly.

"Oh," Jewell said, taken aback. She recovered quickly—she hadn't been brought up by Charles Whittington to be unskilled at dinner-table conversation. "We must have never run into each other. Fancy that in such a small town."

"Oh, yes, we ran into each other a lot."

"We did?"

"I worked with Sam while I was in high school," Clay said, smiling lazily.

*He's enjoying this,* Jewell thought with increasing panic. *I'm looking like a complete fool, and he's loving every minute of it.*

"Sam?" she asked, trying to put the right intonation on her words so that it sounded as if there were a hundred Sams that each of them might know. "Which Sam?"

"Your gardener."

"I remember now. You, um, did wonderful work."

"You don't remember at all," Clay corrected.

"Okay, I don't remember," she admitted. "But you couldn't have been at the house all that often. I would have noticed."

"Every afternoon at four. Stayed till ten. And Saturdays and Sundays. For three years."

"Why, that's nearly full-time work! When was this?"

"During high school. I had a family to support."

She looked quizzically at him.

"Two brothers, three sisters," Clay explained. "My father ran off when I was twelve. My mother worked as a waitress—she needed me to do my share."

"Sounds like you did a lot more than just your share."

He shrugged and leaned back as a waiter discreetly took their plates, his empty and hers untouched.

"I did what I had to do," he said.

"Does that mean we were in high school together?" Jewell asked.

"I'm not sure. When did you graduate?"

"Ten years ago."

"You were a few years behind me. But we left school the same year. I never finished my senior year."

"You never graduated?"

"Couldn't afford to. Had bills to pay."

Jewell sighed and looked out on the river at a passing paddleboat. Here she was sitting at dinner with a man who pumped gas for a living, who was a high-school dropout, who probably didn't have a cent to his name.

And yet, while yesterday she would have thought herself his superior, today she could barely call herself his equal.

She studied him covertly, a sidelong glance from beneath thick lashes. He had been nothing more than a tool—a means to fix her car, to get her on her way—nothing better than any other servant to the Whittington money.

Now, suddenly, she was aware of the man—a man she wouldn't have given a second thought to a day ago.

And he was a man unlike any other that she had ever known.

Rough, callused hands. Brutally chiseled jaw. Dark eyes that were deceptively boyish and yet shimmering with manly passion and wisdom. And a nose that tilted ever so slightly to the right, making Jewell wonder if there were battles in his past that were bloody and ugly.

She felt something mischievous, something downright wicked, about the impulse she had to touch him, to make him touch her. To reach across the table—here, in L'Hermitage, no less, nearly as sacred as church—to take his broad hand and . . .

She had had satisfying, if tepid, relations with Winfield—on the rare occasions when both were in town and both were available and both were in the mood. She had thought that was the way proper romances should be—a notion that Winfield did nothing to dispel. And she had called it "inappropriate"—never coming right out with the word *sleazy*—when some of her girlfriends had taken a "walk on the wild side" with the tennis pro at the country club or one of the summer help at their homes.

And now, in as desperate straits as she was, she was actually considering him!

But she couldn't. Absolutely couldn't. Because each of her girlfriends had known the security of wealth. Romances ended, and her girlfriends could escape messy entanglements with ease. Tennis pros were fired under mysterious circumstances, summer help returned to whatever Yankee state they came from, gardeners and handymen were summarily dismissed.

And good daughters married well and safely, their transgressions forgiven, if not entirely forgotten.

And they could afford this because they had all the security of their trust funds and their family money.

The sons of good families did the same thing, although perhaps more openly.

Jewell shivered as she returned Clay's dead-on look. There wasn't any place to run to, any sanctuary or protection if she shared his bed, no boundary that she could put up between them, no safety net. She couldn't make a single phone call to have him blacklisted at every employer in the area if she tired of him. She couldn't dismiss him with one hand while dialing the phone number of a more respectable suitor with the other. She couldn't escape the consequences if she shared his bed.

If she played now, she played for keeps.

So, of course, she reasoned, better not to play at all.

Because she was too good for this—too good for Clay, too good for the life he would offer, too good for the shambles that would be left when they came apart.

At least, that's how she'd always been raised.

Too good.

As Clay's study of her lingered, first at her body and then directly in her eyes, Jewell had the distinct impression he understood what kind of calculations she made.

"Why don't you tell me a little more about how you ended up here tonight?" he asked neutrally.

She bit her lip. Harder than she intended.

At first, she thought she'd deflect his question—a Southern belle was raised to know how to talk for hours without revealing a single nugget of information.

Then she realized discretion didn't matter. Everyone knew. Maybe Clay would be the only one who would know the whole truth.

"My father died. He had been sick for ages, so it was more a blessing than anything else," she said, and she nodded at his murmur of sympathy. "He had cancer, but the final blow was a heart attack. He left all his money to my half brother, who runs a homeless shelter."

"That came as a surprise?"

"Yes. The will said he wanted to teach me independence, self-reliance and a few other skills, and that's supposed to be the reason for leaving me broke and my brother wealthy."

"But your brother's going to use it for the homeless," Clay said. "That's not exactly the same as making him a wealthy man."

Jewell felt a familiar defensiveness.

"You're just like Thomas Fogerty, my father's lawyer. And even Rev. Copland. All of you think my brother is a saint and that this is a wonderful thing for my father to have done."

"I didn't say anything like that," Clay said. "But now that you say that, I guess I agree. Why shouldn't your father's money go to help the homeless?"

Jewell sighed. Maybe she shouldn't have confided in him. Where she would expect to find sympathy, she found he couldn't understand. Probably because he had never had money, so he didn't know what it meant to lose it all.

And also because he had never known her father.

"My father has never talked about the homeless, never talked about leaving his money to charity, never indicated that that's what he'd like to do with his money. Besides, my brother—sorry, half brother—has been in and out of trouble all his life, and I find it hard to believe that he's suddenly a saint out helping the needy."

"People can change," Clay said gently. "I think it's very noble to want to help the less fortunate—your brother and father are both doing their bit."

"You think I sound like a spoiled brat, don't you?" Jewell accused dismally.

"A little," Clay conceded. "Still, it must have been a shock. All your life, expecting to be taken care of, and suddenly finding out you have to make it on your own."

Jewell wasn't sure whether he was being sarcastic or sympathetic.

"How does the fiancé figure in all this?" Clay asked. "I mean, the Sims family is pretty wealthy. A few million to give the poor a break shouldn't make any difference to you if you're married into the Sims family."

"Winfield broke up with me this afternoon under pressure from his family. They're concerned because I don't bring any of my own money into the marriage. Apparently they're having tougher times than anyone is aware of. They were counting on the Whittington money coming into the family when we wed. They had hoped my father would put together a trust fund, because Winfield really is like me—he can't work. I mean, he has a job as a lawyer in town, but it's really just a place for him to spend a few hours a day."

"In at ten, out by four?" Clay prompted.

"Yeah, with a two-hour lunch thrown in," Jewell said. "Anyhow, he tried to be gentle, but it still was pretty awful."

"Wimp."

"That's what I said."

They shared a tentative smile.

"So what are you going to do?" Clay asked.

"Go back to my father's lawyer and try to fight the will, I guess."

"Why?"

"Why? There are millions of dollars at stake here."

"But why don't you just do what your father wanted? Learn some independence, self-reliance. Get a job. Support yourself. Stand on your own two feet."

Jewell shook her head. "I can't believe my father would have blindsided me this way," she said crisply. "I know I've been robbed of my birthright somehow and I'm not going to let it happen. My father was wrong to do what he did. Maybe he wasn't in his right mind when he wrote the will. Maybe he was pressured into it somehow. Maybe the will isn't even one that he wrote."

"But I might have done the same thing myself," Clay said quietly. "Made my children learn to stand on their own two feet."

"Why?"

"I've never had a child, so I'm not completely sure how I'd feel. But I raised my brothers and sisters. I bought them all the necessities for school, even some luxuries I never had for myself and thought were pretty silly at the time. You know, sweet-sixteen parties and the prom and two weeks during the summer at overnight camp. But all my siblings have a college degree and a job, and I think that's all a parent owes a kid. Good upbringing, some lessons in right and wrong, a chance to get an education, and then I think a kid has to make it on his own."

"You don't understand anything about what I'm going through," Jewell said, her anger swelling. Clay was an easy target, easier than facing the facts. But he was also insufferable, with a definite point of view. A wrong point of view. "You don't understand this problem at all. It has nothing to do with making sacrifices for your children or raising them right. I was robbed. I don't know how, but I don't forget for a moment that I was robbed."

She shocked herself with a forcefulness she didn't often display. They both were silent for a moment— her lips pressed firmly together, his strong jaw clenched. He was the first to look away.

"Maybe I don't understand how you feel. But my father left me with a lot less than you've got now. I survived, you can, too."

Jewell looked away from his intense gaze.

He didn't, he couldn't, understand that he had strength.

Strength she was sure she didn't share.

Strength to survive.

Jewell needed her money back, she needed her house back, she needed her security back.

She wished she could have her father back. Just to talk one last time. If he meant to leave her nothing material, then so be it. But she wanted to hear his voice. She still couldn't believe she'd never see him again.

"You know," Clay added, "you could just get yourself a different fiancé. A wealthy one. One with a little office in town to keep him out of the house for a few hours a day."

"Well, Clay, darlin', you have solved my little problem," Jewell exclaimed lightly. She fixed a honey-sweet smile on her face, one that gently but firmly put him in his place. "I just might do that. Now, why don't we just enjoy our fine meal?"

She steered the conversation quickly away from the dangerous personal waters, launching into a long explanation of the antebellum origins of the mansion that had been converted to a five-star restaurant, the chef's international training, the restaurant's racier Prohibition days.

Jewell wasn't about to continue any discussion about her birthright—gone; her future—uncertain; her feelings about her father—shock; and her capacity for living on her own—probably nonexistent.

One thing she knew for certain—she was Jewell Whittington of the Pontchartreaux estate.

And she would go back there one day.

She would live there again as its mistress.

She would get her birthright back because she knew deep in her bones that her father had never meant for her to be here.

She smiled pleasantly at her dinner partner and thought to herself that no matter how sexy, how handsome, how undeniably tempting he might be on some primitive level, she and Clay wouldn't get any closer, would always be separated by at least twenty-five inches of linen, bone china, glittering crystal and ornate silver—would be kept apart by invisible lines of class and wealth that Clay couldn't even see.

## Chapter Three

Clay concentrated on his *crème brûlée*—a fancy-named custard with a gently burned caramel top that had been so sweet and delicate when it was presented to him. Now it seemed overbearing.

He could see her humiliation coming, but was powerless to stop it. And he wanted to stop it, because during dinner she had become so real to him, so vitally human, so filled with anguish. As misplaced and selfish as he thought it was to fight against a man's last will and final wishes, she didn't deserve what was about to happen.

He couldn't stop the destruction of her fortune, but he could discreetly pretend to be unaware of the extent of her downfall.

"*M'selle,* your card has been denied," Henri whispered at Jewell's ear.

Clay looked up, caught Henri's eye and frowned, trying to signal, man-to-man, that he would work out the bill.

But Henri's glance darted away, and Clay realized with a stab that the tiny maître d' was actually enjoying being the bearer of such news.

Clay clenched his jaw, steadying himself from the desire to settle the bill with his fist.

Better to watch how the princess handled this first crisis of her new life as a regular gal.

She paled, took a deep breath and swallowed hard.

"Why?" she whispered back to Henri.

"The company explains the card has been canceled," Henri explained, his French accent slipping only slightly at the mention of something so base as credit trouble. "I'm sure there is only some *petit* problem, but I have regretfully been instructed by the company to cut the card in half and mail the two pieces to them. Would you perhaps have another method of payment?"

By the time he reached the final question, Henri's Southern roots were firmly in place and Clay was ready to throttle him.

Still, Clay said nothing.

Watch her, he told himself.

Watch her deal with it.

She'll have to learn someday, a voice within him warned, and while you may often be the last resort of stray dogs, lost children and the dirt poor, you don't have to take on Jewell Whittington, as well.

Clay leaned back in his chair and now regarded Henri with a frank, steady stare.

The maître d' backed two steps away from the table and, as if marking out a line in the sand, crossed his arms over his chest and waited.

Taking a deep, ragged breath, Jewell fished in her purse and pulled out her wallet. She handed Henri a Platinum Visa card.

"Try this," she said.

Henri granted Clay a triumphant smirk and took the card.

As Henri retreated, she smiled nervously at Clay.

"Michael must have called American Express," she said with as little outrage as she could manage. "But we'll try Visa."

"What happens if Visa doesn't work?"

Her eyes blinked, and Clay realized just how bad of a question it was.

She was facing the abyss for the first time in her life, and even if he thought she had been spoiled and shielded for far too long, he had to sympathize with her a little. Just a little. She hadn't been prepared for adversity. He imagined she watched the nightly news and said, *Those terrible things happen to other people, not me.*

And that was exactly how Charles Whittington had wanted it, Clay thought to himself. Clay had watched, from a distance, how Whittington coddled and spoiled his little darling. Birthdays were celebrated with the extravagance of national holidays—celebrities flown in on the Whittington jet. The trips to every corner of the globe—she danced in Rio for Carnivale, she walked in the Easter parade in New York and she summered mostly in France. The dresses bought straight out of magazines, so many that Clay was certain she never wore the same one twice.

And every fad and fashion was satisfied. Ballet, tap dance, swimming pools. Even private lessons from Olympic-quality athletes for every sport she took an interest in.

Many were surprised when Jewell didn't marry within the customary two years of her coming-out party. Not Clay. He had been put into use as a waiter for the elegant ball and, between serving caviar and champagne to the guests, he had studied Jewell in the Whittington ballroom. Ethereally beautiful, her white gown as sumptuous at its multilayered hem as it was scanty at its décolletage, she danced with a movie star, a rising young member of the White House administration, a steel heir from Philadelphia and three members of a South American polo team.

Through every lilting, romantic turn, she did all the right things—and looked bored.

Clay could feel and see her boredom even as those whom she had been taught to play hostess to were fooled.

She didn't find a husband that year—although many men longed for her. She didn't find a husband the next year or the next. Some said her problem was that no man could live up to Daddy. Some said her problem was that she was too picky. Some said her problem was that she fell under the spell of education—jumping from one subject to another, never satisfied to graduate and do something "useful" with her life.

But "useful" was not what she had been raised for.

She'd have to learn pretty quick, Clay thought.

There it was again—torn, wanting to take her into his arms and comfort her and maybe even kiss her with tenderness, and then wanting to despise her, to throw the roughness of life in her face. Tell her that she was only dealing with what others, even he, faced every day.

And then kiss that mouth as if to teach her a lesson about real men. And real women.

"Don't worry about the money," he advised from across the table. "Just put it out of your mind. You have to learn to worry about the things that happen when they happen and not a moment before. Now, you were telling me about silverware."

Actually, silverware only mildly interested him, but he suspected that she thought the subject was very dull when she really wanted to have a good worry, and maybe even a cry, over what was happening with her money.

Her daddy's money.

But she gamely tried to keep Clay entertained.

The truth was, everything she talked about was information that he had never learned. If it couldn't be found in the public library, if it couldn't be acquired through hard work—Clay was at sea. But he was determined to learn. Everything. Every nuance of the world that he would enter, was entering, would enter, was his if he worked hard.

"My favorite pattern is Francis I," Jewell said, trying her best to keep her mind on the topic. If this guy wanted to hear about silverware, she had an obligation as hostess to give him what he wanted even if the information was probably worthless to him. "Francis I is really a series of sixteen different flower-and-vine designs brought together as one. Woodrow Wilson was the first president to use it in the White House. It was the favorite pattern of Wilson, Roosevelt and Eisenhower. Most folks 'round here use the Chantilly pattern and put the bride's monogram on the base of the knife handle, but I've always thought the Francis I had a real good feel to it. The handles are more substantial, weightier, and give a dinner guest a feeling of luxury."

Silverware, Oriental rugs, French and German wines, crystal patterns, proper seating for a cotillion dinner, how to chose among invitations for Magnolia Night. Clay kept her talking nonstop, filing away every bit of information that she possessed.

"What kind of china goes with Francis I?" he asked.

"I've always been partial to Grasmere pattern because the rim mirrors the flowers on the base of the silver."

She studied him carefully. "Clay, why do you want to know all this?"

He looked away. "You think I'm never going to use any of this information, don't you?" he asked. "And you think it's worthless to teach me."

She was startled by his intensity, but that was exactly what she had been thinking.

"Clay, to get a full set of silver costs thousands of dollars. And if you're going to spend that much on silverware, you should get china that's going to look good with it. Real bone china. That's another several thousand. Then there's crystal. You know, glasses."

"I know what crystal is," he said quietly.

"Point is, Clay, it can cost ten thousand dollars to lay down a nice table for a few friends, and that's before you even buy your napkins."

"Paper, of course."

She laughed and, when she saw his answering smile, she relaxed.

"Oh, Clay, you've been stringing me along. I bet you're just trying to keep my mind off my troubles," she said with practiced breathlessness. Clay suspected that she herself was the one more determined to keep the conversation off the potential land mines of her life. "I must sound like I'm talking about a different planet—silverware and fine wines and huge parties," she added.

"Yeah, it might be another planet, but you're a beautiful alien," Clay said, the playfully seductive words out of his mouth before he thought better.

Jewell smiled ruefully. "I'm not in the market, Clay," she said crisply. A little too crisply.

"You're not in the market for a man like me," he corrected gently. "It's all right, there's no reason you should be."

She started to protest, but stopped as Henri returned—shaking his head.

"*M'selle,* I have again been asked to confiscate your Visa card. Perhaps..." He let his eyes linger on Clay.

"Oh, no, this is my treat, and I'm going to have to figure out a way to pay," Jewell said frantically. She bit her lip and fixed a look of Southern graciousness upon Henri, a look that was hard for any man to refuse. "Could I give you an I.O.U.?"

Henri recoiled as if she had just insulted all of France.

"You'll take an I.O.U., right, Henri?" Clay demanded firmly.

Henri sputtered a reply, dangerously close to forever ruining his reputation as a Frenchman of refined elegance. Clay stood up and took Henri's collar into his hands.

"You will, won't you, Henri?"

Clay held him for only an instant, but the audible gasp among the diners at surrounding tables lingered for long minutes.

Henri felt the bills slip from Clay's nimble fingers into the inside pocket of his white dinner jacket. He gulped and mentally calculated the worth of the bulge. Then he smiled at Jewell with faint Gallic grace as he patted down his lapel.

"We would be delighted to take your I.O.U., *m'selle.*"

As Henri left with Jewell's scrawled promise to repay, she leaned forward to confront Clay.

"You shouldn't have threatened him," she said. "That wasn't very nice. You embarrassed me and probably frightened that poor man to death. He's from France, you know, and isn't used to that sort of thing. Came over to this country only a few years ago, and we're lucky to have lured such a man all the way from his birthplace."

Clay figured Henri's birthplace was no more than twenty miles away from where they sat. But enough of Jewell's illusions had been shattered for one day.

"Sorry," he said with an apologetic shrug.

He stood up and was about to help her from her own seat, but she was already gone—gliding across the dining room with regal grace, a nod and a smile for every openmouthed stare from a diner. Clay had no choice but to follow her.

In the lobby, Henri bowed a polite goodbye and, as Clay passed, he took the borrowed sport coat back.

"Fifty says she doesn't even kiss you good night," Henri whispered to Clay in his familiar accent.

"I don't bet on horses, card games or ladies," Clay replied evenly. "I would suggest you don't do so, either."

Henri backed away, sensing the dangerous undercurrent of Clay's words.

Clay shrugged away the confining jacket and ran to catch up with Jewell.

"I'm going to drop off the car at the station," he said as he got into the cab of the tow truck. "Where can I take you?"

Jewell took a deep breath.

"I'm not sure," she admitted. "I don't have any money for a hotel, and now it looks as if I don't have any credit cards, either."

"What about friends? Surely, someone's got room for you for a few days, till you get on your feet."

"Friends?" Jewell chuckled.

"If they're good friends, they wouldn't mind."

"Clay, I got a confession to make."

"Yeah?"

"My friends seem to be unavailable."

"You mean, nobody's got a room for you?"

She visibly shuddered at his blunt words. "No, it's nothing like that. Mindy, Genie and Arianna are at the Heart Association Ball and Georgann said she would but her mother-in-law is coming in this evening and, well, you know how it is..." Her voice, which had started off so assuredly, faltered and finally she was silent.

"Right," Clay said. "Unavailable."

He started up the engine, leaning his head back against the headrest.

Stray dogs, lost children, the down-and-out—and now Jewell Whittington.

He could only blame himself if he ended up regretting what he was about to do.

He took a deep breath. "Why don't you spend the night with me? I use an apartment on the second floor of the station. You can sleep on my bed, and I'll sleep on the couch. Scout's honor, I won't do anything."

"Are you sure?" She pounced on the offer, quickly adding, "It will only be for the night. I'm sure by tomorrow morning I'll have a more permanent place. I'm sure Mindy would be especially delighted to take me in—she owes me, you know, I introduced her to her husband. He and I almost got engaged. And I'm not entirely without friends. Even if I don't have a dime to my name, I've still got my friends."

Both of them wondered in the heavy, humid silence whether any of those friends would come through for her now that the Whittington money wasn't there.

As they drove through the rain, Jewell envisioned the rustic charm of the apartment in which Clay lived—pine furniture, hand-sewn quilts, soothing chintz armchairs, delicate lace café curtains. Somehow, she also let her hopes overcome realism by adding a hot tub—perhaps tucked up on a porch off the main bedroom. She would slip into the soothing water—by herself, of course—and try to wash the troubles of the day away.

Surely, after a relaxing soak and a good night's sleep, tomorrow wouldn't be nearly so frightening to consider.

As Clay pulled into the parking spot behind the garage, she thanked him again for his hospitality—but he reminded her that the apartment might be a little shabby by her standards.

"Oh, I'm sure I'll like it just fine," she said, envisioning a down mattress and fluffy pillows.

How she had let her imagination take such a fancy, Jewell couldn't have explained, except by some dint of wishful thinking.

When Clay unlocked the door at the top of the narrow fire escape, Jewell quivered with anticipation.

And then she closed her eyes, willing reality to cede to her will.

She opened her eyes.

The apartment stubbornly remained what it was.

"I knew you'd be a little disappointed," Clay said softly.

"Oh, no," she protested limply.

There was a worn brown sofa. Two chairs on either side of a wood table. A dilapidated armoire and an iron bed. A plain blue comforter. Whitewashed shutters.

And two mutts who climbed off the bed with all the indignation of purebreds. They mistrustfully circled her as she stood in the center of the room.

Neat, clean, but completely devoid of charm or grace.

How could anybody live like this? she wondered.

There was only one pleasant surprise—something she never would have anticipated, even if she had driven hundreds of miles and had had hours to decorate and redecorate Clay's apartment in her head.

Books. Hundreds of them. All over the place. Stacked in corners, lined up in rows, stacked beside the couch like an occasional table.

As Jewell toured the room, she fingered the covers and discovered quickly they were about everything. Archaeology. Physics. Mathematics. Architecture. Business.

"What do you do with these things?" she asked, picking up a hardcover second-edition Charles Dickens.

"I read them."

"You do?"

"Yeah, don't look so surprised," he said, gently taking the book and returning it to its place on a scrubbed pine shelf.

She looked on the shelves again. "You've read *Pride and Prejudice*," she said, pointing to the shelf that featured authors whose last names began with *A*.

"And I think it's a romantic comedy about a family in England," Clay said.

She shook her head, smiling briefly at his reference to her master's thesis.

He couldn't help it if he were naive—and she did have to admire his efforts at educating himself.

"What about this?" she asked, pointing to *David Copperfield*.

"A book about a boy who works hard."

"And you don't think of it as a commentary on the horrible condition of the poor working class in England?" she teased.

He shrugged. "There's poor people everywhere. David Copperfield was a good kid. He worked hard. He was nice to people. That's what counts. Besides, the book was fun."

"Fun?"

"Yeah, fun to read. Sometimes, the worth of a book is just whether it's a good read."

"But—"

"I know. Not very intellectual of me, is it?"

She opened her mouth to speak, changed her mind and then closed her mouth.

"I think you think too much," Clay said.

She backed away into a shelf of books, sending several volumes tumbling.

"Please stop acting like I'm about to pounce on you," he said.

She opened her mouth to protest, and then clamped her lips together into a prim line. His full lower lip hardened and curled into a sardonic smile.

"I have a right to know under what conditions your offer of a place to stay has been made," she said more righteously than she intended. She sounded like an indignant virgin—when she knew herself to be a knowledgeable and sophisticated woman.

And yet, was she so sophisticated?

Strange that a hick mechanic could make her feel unsure of herself and so suddenly, too. As if some sexual part of himself had remained hidden but now was out in the open—taunting her now that she was on his turf.

What had been a sweet little pied-à-terre in her imagination was now a predator's lair.

"Under what conditions?" Clay demanded. "You're asking me under what conditions I've brought you here? Are you sure you've never been to law school?"

"I'm sure I would have remembered if I had," she said dryly. "I'll speak more plainly if it'll help, but I'm sure you know exactly what I'm asking. Does your generous offer come with a price tag?''

He jerked his head toward the window—the rain like the drumming of a giant's fingers against the glass.

''Sleeping out there would be preferable to sleeping with me?'' Clay asked. ''Purely hypothetical question, of course.''

''Yes, and that's not a hypothetical answer,'' she said, staring him straight in the eye. Hoping that he didn't see her hesitation, her self-doubt, and—most importantly—her ambivalence about a sexy hunk who was her equal only when society was stripped away.

As it had been today.

Clay hadn't expected an answer to his question.

''Am I that ugly? Am I not refined enough for you?''

Jewell shook her head and laughed. ''No, you know exactly how good-looking you are,'' she said, purposely ignoring his question about refinement. ''But I'm getting my money back, I'm getting my house back and I'm going back to everything I grew up with. I don't want any complications.''

''And there would be complications if we slept together—even once? Just for fun? A one-night stand?''

''Even once. Complications.''

''You don't want complications like having to say 'hi' if you passed me on the street? I would have thought you would like an adventure story to share with your girlfriends—when you return to the protection of your castle.''

He put his palms against the bookshelf, boxing her in.

"Clay..." she protested, but her mouth dried and her words came out more like a moan of desire than an order to step back.

"You don't want complications like a rumor about me interfering with a suitable man paying court to you. You don't want complications like..."

Jewell swallowed. "Enough!"

She slipped out from under his arm.

Clay turned around and leaned his head against the shelf.

"Do you want me to leave?" she asked, pointing to the window.

He closed his eyes. From the rag rug at the end of the bed, he heard the thin whine of Samson and the answering grumble of Delilah. He had found Samson, reasonably healthy but hungry as all get-out, abandoned on one of the back roads. Delilah had come later, and her limp still reminded him of the weeks Clay had nursed her back to health from a hit-and-run accident. Now, it seemed, the dogs were encouraging him to take in yet another stray—a decidedly ungracious one.

"You take the bed, I'll take the couch," he said. "But you have to share with Samson and Delilah."

She opened her mouth to protest, but reconsidered as the dogs confidently returned to their positions at the edge of the bed. They were her allies, she decided. They were evidence of Clay's soft spot.

A soft spot that kept her out of the rain.

Clay enjoyed watching her struggle with and finally accept defeat on the issue of sleeping with dogs. But she wasn't completely vanquished.

"I'm going to take a bath," she announced. "I've been looking forward to that for a while. Do you mind?"

He shook his head. "Go on," he said. "I'll alert the media that the princess is bathing."

Jewell grumbled but held her tongue. This was not the time to argue—she needed a bath, a good night's sleep, and tomorrow morning a few phone calls and she'd be out of here.

A BATH, particularly a hot one, made all the difference in a woman's thinking, Jewell decided later as she tensed and relaxed her toes beneath the surface of the bubbles.

She pushed away thoughts of her father because it was just too overwhelming. Instead, she tried to persuade herself that things could not be as bad as all that. Sure, Michael had thrown her a curve, but she would recover. Besides, it was still possible that Thomas Fogerty, her father's lawyer, would figure out a way around the will. If he didn't, she'd find a lawyer who would. And she would live with Mindy for a few weeks, perhaps offer to take care of the baby for a few hours a day. And remember to send a spectacular floral arrangement as thanks when she left their guest apartment for Pontchartreaux. Jewell congratulated herself on her generosity and utter correctness.

She heard the soft rustle of fabric as Clay changed the sheets in the next room. A good night's sleep would give her the energy to face her problems head-on. She was certain that everything was going to be straightened out very quickly. She would have her house back. Would have her whole life back.

She was troubled only by a niggling sense of guilt about Clay.

Because you didn't sleep with him? A voice in her head asked.

No, because I wanted to, she thought.

Any woman would.

Even now, as she rolled over onto her side—feeling the slippery water like a warm caress—she knew she could call him into the bathroom. Apologize. Reach out her hand to him. Watch him undress. Quickly. He would do it quickly. He would enter the bathtub carefully, though, excited and grateful for her invitation. He would roll her over to be on top of him, and he would worship her breasts and legs, seeking permission at every caress, permission for his next move. And then, the tables would turn, and he would be less a supplicant than an aggressor. His animal instincts would take over, and he would...

"Wait a minute," Jewell said aloud. "What am I thinking of?"

What was she thinking of? She had lost her father, lost her house, lost her money and lost her life-style—and she was fantasizing about some mechanic who might be a brute but who had had enough common decency to give her a room for the night?

A gift, she thought.

A small, tasteful gift to Clay would be appropriate to show her appreciation for the use of his apartment. Maybe a thousand-dollar check. Generous enough that he couldn't come back to her for more. Small enough to make clear it was gratitude and not blackmail. And cash was just perfect to let him know that the use of his apartment was all she had taken from him, all she had wanted from him.

"I think I've figured out what to do, Clay!" Jewell called from the bathtub. "Tomorrow, I'll go down to Cherise Salon. That's where I buy most of my clothes, and I'll just ask Cherise to give me a job. I'm sure she'll be happy to have me. I know all about fashion and how to dress. It would be a real treat for her to hire me. Know what I mean? And the money would tide me over until this legal stuff gets straightened out. And maybe instead of living with Mindy, I'll live with the Fogerty family—the father has been my own father's personal lawyer for years and he'd be glad to take me. And that way, I can keep a closer eye on the legal stuff. Because I know my father never meant to..."

She didn't hear any response to her brainstorming.

"Clay?"

She reluctantly stepped out of the tub and pulled a towel around her. She opened the door a crack.

"Clay?"

She looked at the bed. The sheets were worn, but crisply laundered, sweet smelling and perfectly tucked. The cornflower blue comforter was worn and graying, but it was soothingly plump.

The bed, and the man in it, were very inviting.

But he was asleep.

Clay sat unconscious, his head slumped against the ornate iron headboard, as if he had said to himself that he would rest but a moment. Sprawled near his feet, Samson and Delilah stared up at her without lifting their heads.

Dropping the towel on the floor, Jewell opened the armoire and looked at the clothes hung up inside.

She pulled on a soft white polo shirt from the top shelf of the armoire and a pair of boxers from the drawer beneath. Then she sat down on the couch, watching Clay's rising and falling chest.

He was handsome, no doubt about it, with a primitive sexuality that could make most women forget all propriety.

But Jewell was not most women.

She tried the couch.

It was uncomfortable, with upholstery fabric that had tiny metallic threads that hurt like the dickens about five seconds after she lay down.

That bed, that bed, looked so much more comfortable. Even with two dogs cuddled up against each other.

"Clay, wake up," she said.

Nothing.

Samson and Delilah lifted their heads, looked at their master and then put their heads back down and closed their eyes.

"Clay," she said more insistently. "Wake up. You said I could have the bed."

She shook his shoulder. Without rousing, he settled more deeply into the bed, turning on his side. She lifted one of his arms and let it drop. He didn't stir.

"Oh, hell," she said, and walked around to the other side of the bed.

She slipped between the sheets and jammed her toes into what little space was left by the dogs.

She had never slept with a man before—at least in the restful sense of the word. Not even Winfield Sims IV. He felt it just wouldn't be proper since he lived in the *garçonière* to his parents' house.

Now, not even twelve hours after she was un-engaged to one man, she was in bed—at least, for the purposes of sleep—with another.

"Not for long," she whispered to herself. "Not for long."

She closed her eyes and tried to fall asleep by thinking of her home, thinking of her return, thinking of her reclaiming her way of life. But her mind continually returned to thoughts of her father, of her fiancé, of all that she had lost, of all that she missed so terribly.

She couldn't sleep. Her thoughts tortured her. The dogs crowded against her, and their thin snores punctured the silence. The light from the neon sign outside annoyed her. And Clay...

He rolled over and flung his arm around her waist, pulling her to him like a spoon. Her back splayed against him, she could feel his erection grow against her and then subside as he fell into ever deeper sleep. His arm grew heavier on the soft space of flesh between her hip bone and ribs.

"Clay, wake up right this minute," she whispered.

Samson looked once at her, challenging her to protest as he slipped into the remaining few inches of the bed.

She was trapped. Between dog and man.

She'd never fall asleep.

She picked up Clay's hand and rested it more comfortably on her thigh. She absently patted Samson, who rolled over regally to grant her permission to scratch his stomach.

And within seconds, she was out.

## Chapter Four

The blow to his head woke him instantly.

"What the...?" he shouted reflexively, throwing one arm over his head before the second strike. He grabbed his assailant and then, as his hands squeezed soft flesh, let go of her as quickly as he would a vicious cottonmouth.

Falling back into the warm comfort of his pillow, he squinted up at Jewell. The blinding sunlight, the shimmering blond of her hair, the striking white of his T-shirt covering her breasts and the stinging of his head where she'd brained him—it was too much for him.

He groaned, closed his eyes and shoved his face into the pillow.

"What's going on?" he murmured. "Why do you torture me like this? What've I ever done to you."

"Get off the bed," she ordered.

He looked up. "Are you talking to me? 'Cause this is my bed."

"No, I'm talking to the dogs."

He looked at Samson and Delilah, who padded off the bed with wheezing reluctance.

"Don't talk in that tone of voice to them," Clay warned.

"Well, don't you touch me. Those dogs just give you a shield so you can grope me. You think I don't know it's your hands, but I do."

"Dream on, Princess, I have no intention of touching you."

"You were."

"My mistake."

"You were fondling me."

"Jewell, I'm too tired to fondle you."

"Well, you were doing it in your sleep."

"That's the only way it would ever happen," Clay muttered to the pillow.

"What'd you say?"

"Nothing. Just let me go back to sleep."

"It's time to get up."

"What time is it?" he grumbled, pushing his face back into the pillow.

"Nine o'clock."

"I'm going back to sleep," Clay said. "I've had five hours' rest if I'm lucky—with you rolling around. And I worked a forty-eight-hour shift this weekend."

"Don't you open at six?"

"Did you hear anybody honking their horn? If somebody needs something, they know how to get me. And there's only one car in the garage. Yours."

"So why aren't you working on it? I need to get into town."

He lifted his head up. "You have a lot of nerve."

She paled and Clay shook his head. He was going to be stuck with her all morning if she didn't have wheels.

"You can use the pickup today," he said. "Keys are on the kitchen table."

Jewell glanced at the kitchenette against the wall. Without remorse, he lifted his head to stare after her. Even with her wearing his boxers, she couldn't conceal the curved hips and the long legs. She swiped the keys from the table and headed for the bathroom.

He groaned languorously.

Too bad she thought she was too good for him.

"I assume you're getting out today!" he called out over the sound of the shower. "Getting a place to stay with one of your friends. Could you remember to get the truck back here when you do?"

He shook his head.

Unlikely.

At least he had her car hostage.

He laid his head back into his pillow and welcomed the two dogs back up into their accustomed spots. He must have dozed, because the next thing he knew, Jewell stood over him, her hair pulled severely from her face, one of his own T-shirts topping her black skirt.

"I'm going to get a job," she announced proudly. "My first one. If you don't count volunteer work at the hospital or cochairing the Cancer Society Ball."

"Congratulations," Clay said blandly. "I got my first one when I was twelve. Now, can I go back to sleep?"

"Just one question. What's the best way to get a job? I want to get one nailed down today. I have a feeling it'll take a few weeks, maybe months, to get back to Pontchartreux, but until then, I guess I'll have to work. And I'm thinking I should have a fallback position in case Cherise, the lady who owns the clothes store, doesn't take me.''

Clay stared at her openmouthed. "You know, Jewell, you know so much about a lot of things. But I'm getting the impression that most of it is just plain useless. You have never asked for a job?"

"No."

"Do you know how to pump gas?"

"No."

"Do you know how to wash your clothes at a Laundromat?"

"No."

"Do you know how to plant cotton?"

"No."

"Do you know how to read a classified ad?"

"No."

"Well, then, Jewell, I hope you get your money back because I swear you can't survive without it."

"Clay, I am not stupid!"

"I know you're not stupid. Last night, you explained a whole passel of things to this ignorant fool. Silverware. Giving parties. Buying the finest linens. And every one of those fields of expertise requires money. So maybe you are more deserving than the homeless—they're used to deprivation. You're not."

She shrieked in frustration, grabbed a pillow and was ready to brain him again. But Samson and Delilah roused themselves to menace her.

Only Clay knew the two dogs were cowards.

"Damn you, Clay, I am getting a job this morning. And I'm getting my money back. My father would have wanted it that way."

"Whatever."

With a prim set of her lips, she turned from him, pulling his windbreaker from the armoire.

"You think I'm just a spoiled brat about this money, but my father never would have cut me off like this," she said coldly. "He loved me."

"Love isn't the same thing as money."

They stared at each other in silence for some minutes.

"Just tell me how to get a job."

"Find a place with a Help Wanted sign, and go in and ask to see the manager. Ask him if he'll hire you."

"Then what happens?"

"He'll either say yes or no."

Jewell lifted her chin up a little, patted her ponytail and squared her shoulders.

"Next time you see me, Clay, I'm going to have a job, have a place to live with one of my friends and be well on my way to getting my money back."

"I'll be very happy for you," Clay said sardonically. "Now, can I please go back to sleep?"

He closed his eyes and pushed his face far into the pillow. Samson and Delilah sighed and leaned against him—shifting and turning until they each found the most comfortable spot on the bed. Clay heard the clipped sound of her broken-heeled shoes against the tile, and then the door slammed.

"Wish you luck," he whispered, feeling a pang of sympathy. He expected to see her again, all right, but somehow, he didn't think she was going to be too happy to see him.

Sometimes, life at the bottom got a whole lot worse before you started the long climb back up.

"No," SAID CHERISE at the dress shop.

"Sorry, no," said Armand at the hairdresser's.

"No," said the Russian woman at the nail salon.

"No, 'fraid not," said Joe at the health club.

There were so many noes in her day that Jewell decided to treat herself to lunch at the Shakespeare Café—but then remembered she had only sixteen dollars to her name and so she went, for the very first time in her life, to the Depot, a diner by the railroad tracks.

She spent $6.78 on the chicken salad, a piece of cherry pie and a Diet Coke—and left a dollar tip. The rest of her money she converted to quarters and squandered at the pay phone in the back of the kitchen.

Five dollars in change later, she had an even bigger collection of noes. Genie Andrews was out of town. Alice was getting her nails done. Ann Bender was at Moms and Tots with little Charlie. Jewell had to leave a message for Arianna Boyer, who had an answering machine instead of a maid to pick up the phone. And Mindy, upon whom she had rested most of her hopes, had been called out of town unexpectedly according to the maid.

The list went on, through the rest of the alphabet. Not a single friend took her phone call, and Jewell had the sneaking suspicion that many housekeepers were under instructions to lie about their respective mistress's whereabouts.

Jewell didn't want to believe it, but it seemed her own friends were unwilling to talk to her.

These were the friends who would have gladly come to Pontchartreaux manor for a dinner party at a moment's notice, would have had her in their homes to reciprocate an invitation and would have kissed the air next to her cheek at every reception to benefit the hospital, the school, the church or the Cancer Society.

When Jasmine Zielinski's maid announced Jasmine was in the greenhouse and had left instructions not to be disturbed, Jewell gave up.

No, she didn't wish to leave a message.

It would get better at the lawyer's office, no doubt.

Thomas had always had a soft spot for her, hadn't he?

"JEWELL, all of the paperwork is in order," Thomas said sadly. He glanced up to acknowledge his secretary, who had brought a silver tray and set it on a butler's table next to the desk. "I'll serve, Mary."

The secretary discreetly left, closing the door behind her. His fingers uncharacteristically shaking, Thomas poured two cups of coffee and handed Jewell hers.

"But how could he have done this to me?" Jewell wailed, setting the delicate cup and saucer on the desk. "I had no warning. I had always been told that there would be money for me. I had always been told that the house, my house, the house I was raised in, was mine."

"Charles was married before," Thomas reminded her. "And he had a son in that marriage. Michael is just as much Charles's child as you are. Charles has simply chosen to acknowledge him. But he really didn't leave Michael the money—it's going to the homeless shelter."

"Michael has been an embarrassment all his life," Jewell protested.

"I guess Charles thought Michael had finally made something of his life. I knew Michael when he was young," Thomas said, and seemed ready to say more about Michael's early days. Instead, he took a deep breath. "He's a changed man. He's a responsible director of a shelter for the most deserving elements of our society. You have to admire him. And frankly, I think you have to admire Charles."

"Michael is a con man," Jewell said vehemently.

"Now, Jewell, you're just surprised and a little hurt about the will," Thomas soothed.

"I'm not 'just surprised' and a 'little hurt.' I'm totally shocked and I'm incredibly devastated. And you should have known about this will and told me about it."

Thomas paled, and his eyes skittered about the room.

"Okay, okay, I guess it was a surprise to me, too."

"What?" Jewell asked, leaning forward in her seat.

Thomas shrugged his shoulders. "The will was a surprise to me," Thomas admitted, his eyes avoiding hers. "Charles executed it four months ago without consulting me. This doesn't mean the will is invalid. Oh, no, the will is just fine. I just wasn't the one to—"

"But you're his personal attorney," Jewell argued. Her mind raced ahead.

This was her first piece of evidence, other than her own conviction, that something wasn't right about the will. Something that supported her belief that her father hadn't meant to leave her with nothing.

She waited impatiently while Thomas carefully picked his words.

"Jewell, I'm his personal attorney, but don't think that meant Charles didn't do things without consulting me. Many, many business deals were conducted without me having a clue. I was often brought in at the last minute, when the paperwork had to be done."

"But I thought you two did everything together. I heard you came here from Georgia when you were just out of law school. You didn't have a penny to your name and then you met my father."

She looked around the plush office, underscoring the wealth that had come to Thomas Fogerty. Much of it by working for the Whittington family.

"I want a complete investigation into this will," Jewell said.

"No," Thomas said quickly, his hands shaking with emotion. "You're deluding yourself. Dangerously so. Your father left his money to a homeless shelter in Milwaukee. There's nothing illegal, nothing wrong about doing that. In fact, Jewell, it's admirable. I wish more of my clients would do good works with their money."

Jewell shook her head, putting the cup and saucer down heavily on the table.

"I'm getting what's rightfully mine."

"Jewell, I think your father knew you needed to get out on your own or make a commitment to Winfield," Thomas said in measured tones. "You're nearly thirty years old and you've frittered away at college for almost ten years. Your father obviously felt—"

"I have one master's degree and almost have my second. I haven't just frittered away my time."

"My apologies. I misspoke. You have done an excellent job of attaining higher education. But I don't think you've used your education to its complete advantage," he said, warming to his subject. "And I think that's what must have worried Charles."

"So what do you think I should do?"

"Well, I'm sorry about Winfield but I believe you must carry on. Get a job. Get a life. Start from scratch. Plenty of people do. And let Charles's money be used to help the truly deserving."

Jewell gulped. "But I'm not very good at being on my own."

"Not many of us are when we start out," Thomas said softly. "Why don't you go away? Start a new life somewhere else? Your mother's people came from New York, I believe."

"Boston," Jewell corrected.

"Whatever. Someplace up north," he said dismissively. His face brightened. "Why don't you go show some Yankees how to live? They could use some instruction."

"This is my home," Jewell said, surprised at her vehemence. "I won't leave."

Thomas gulped hard and shuffled some papers on his desk.

"Then you'd better make up with your brother," he said harshly. "It's between you and him at this point. Now, I've got a client waiting."

"Thomas, I had one last thing I wanted to ask you," Jewell said.

"What?"

"I need a place to stay," she blurted out. As his eyes narrowed, she rushed on. "Just till I get a job. Just till I figure out what I'm doing. Maybe I can arrange a scholarship with Memphis so I can continue my studies. I'm almost a third of the way through my master's thesis."

Thomas looked away, seeming to concentrate on a pile of papers in front of him.

"Jewell, I'll check with my wife about this, but I think if you're looking for some help, you should go to your brother. This is a family matter, and perhaps Charles thought this will would be the catalyst for a closer relationship between the two of you."

"Michael's the one who threw me out!" Jewell shrieked.

Thomas looked up, startled by her outburst. Mary quietly opened the door to the office and, after a curt nod from Thomas, closed it again.

"I understood that you wanted to leave," Thomas said stiffly. "Michael asked for your help at the homeless shelter. You weren't willing to commit yourself to that."

There it was again. The implication that she was a spoiled brat, a jerk, a selfish . . .

"Don't you think it's very strange that a homeless-shelter director is the one who's making me homeless?" she asked.

Thomas shook his head. "Jewell, go work this out with your brother," he said.

"He's probably the one who has cheated me out of my inheritance!" Jewell cried.

Thomas glared at her, his face flushed and eyes glittering.

"Your father's will was perfectly in order," he said. "Your father left his money to a homeless shelter. You have to learn to accept that. Now, go make peace with Michael."

He stared determinedly at the papers on his desk. She left without saying goodbye.

As she walked through the plushly carpeted hallway, she tried her best to ignore the openmouthed stares of the secretaries at their desks.

In the truck, she faced what she had tried to avoid for twenty-four hours.

Maybe she had to make peace with her half brother.

Maybe there was nothing more to be done.

She drove next to Pontchartreaux and was told by Mia, the housekeeper, that Michael was gone but he had left something for her.

"Where are you staying?" Mia asked her as she led Jewell to the dining room.

Jewell took a deep breath. She had been avoiding thinking about that very question.

"At the gas station."

"Smith's gas station? Good. You are in Clay's hands. He is a very good man. Now I must go. Michael said to give you this."

Jewell sat at the head of the dining-room table, where she had so often overseen dinners and brunches and luncheons. Now all she had in front of her was a single sheet of paper and a business-size envelope. She read the paper's legalese.

I, Jewell Whittington, do voluntarily and without coercion or undue influence, acknowledge the validity of the will of Charles Whittington...

She opened the envelope. Inside was a check, written by Michael on her father's checking account. It was for the amount of twenty thousand dollars.

Tempting, very tempting.

She thought about twenty thousand dollars and all it would buy and all it would bring her. She could fix her car, drive back up to Memphis and finish her master's. She could fly up to Boston, impose herself on some distant relatives and land herself a husband before her money ran out. She could look up a few old boyfriends, the ones who seemed so boring and pompous when she was the Whittington heiress.

Then she ripped up the paper, the check and even the envelope, leaving a pile of scraps on the dining-room table. She let herself out the front door without a goodbye to Mia.

She drove out to the cemetery, squandering her last dollar on a white rose to lay at her parents' grave. The headstone they shared didn't yet record her father's death. She sat down and poured out her troubles, something she had often done when only her mother rested here.

"I miss you," she whispered at last. "I knew it was coming, but oh, God, I miss you. Both of you."

And she knew she always would.

AND THEN THERE WASN'T anyplace else left to go.

At four o'clock, she pulled the pickup into the gas station. Clay was at the cash register. Two cars waited at the garage. The phone rang, again and again. Three men sat on the bench by the door.

"How'd it go?" Clay said, looking up only briefly as he counted out change to a customer.

"Awful," Jewell admitted. "I'm going upstairs to have a nice long cry while I soak my troubles away."

Clay picked up the phone, told whoever it was to hold and accepted the truck's keys from Jewell.

"No, you're not," he said.

"What do you mean, I'm not?"

"You can have your nice long cry and a relaxing bath later. No time for it now. You're hired. Starting now. Know how to use a register?"

Jewell stared at him with undisguised horror. "You want me to work at a gas station? After the kind of day I've had? Besides, me at a gas station? You're joking."

Even as the words left her mouth, she knew that what she wanted to do wasn't as important anymore as what she had to do.

Two more customers—a fat man wearing a T-shirt proclaiming his beer brand of choice and a thinner man in worn overalls—squeezed into the office. They stared at Jewell.

"I'll start you at minimum wage," Clay said, picking the phone back up off the receiver. "You take the register and I'll pump gas. I've got a lady waiting on a new muffler and a—"

"What's minimum wage?"

He told her.

"Forget it. For that kind of money, I couldn't even pay for getting my hair done at the end of the week."

Her audience laughed.

"Lady, that's where we all started," the fat man said. "At the bottom. Minimum wages."

Clay finished his business on the phone, hung up and strode around the counter.

"You don't have any choices, Jewell," he said. "There aren't any free rides."

She stared at him with all the fury that she couldn't direct at her father, at her brother, at the lawyer.

"You're enjoying this, aren't you?" she demanded.

"Enjoying what?"

"My humiliation. Bringing me down. You're enjoying watching everything I've come to expect in my life taken away from me. I sure as hell hope you like the entertainment, Clay, because I swear to God someday I will have everything back. You may think this is funny, but when I'm back in my own house, it won't be so funny to you anymore. I'll be the one laughing."

Clay squared his jaw, and his eyes glazed cold as ice. "I've never thought of hard work as humiliating."

Without another glance in her direction, he walked out to the garage.

"You gonna take my money, lady?" asked the fat man.

"Add a package of Slim Jims, wouldja?" the other said.

Jewell fought tears but slid behind the desk to the cash register.

"I have no idea how to use this thing," she said, exasperated.

"Aw, darlin', don't cry," said the thin man. "I started at minimum wage and now I make nearly double that."

Double minimum wage? Jewell quickly calculated that the man made about what her father had given her each year as a clothing allowance.

She closed her eyes, but that didn't stop the tears from coursing down her cheeks.

The fat man was pragmatic. "Here, you punch in the amount of the gas—that's $14.38—and then you put in my buddy's snack—another seventy-five cents. Then you punch Total and take my money."

Jewell numbly followed his directions.

"This is the worst day of my life," she muttered.

"Hey, that can't be so," said the fat man as he accepted his change. "You got yourself a job and you're working for a good man. What more can you want?"

"Everything," Jewell said as she shut the cash-register drawer. "Everything that's rightfully mine."

AT SEVEN O'CLOCK, after fixing the muffler on Mrs. O'Malley's 1959 Pontiac and helping her into the driver's seat, Clay wiped his hands and walked into the office. Jewell sat on the bench behind the cash register, leaning her head against the cigarette-display board and staring at the ceiling.

"Far as I'm concerned, station's closed," he said, reaching over the counter to open the register drawer. He pulled out a twenty-dollar bill. "Time for a reality check."

Jewell lifted her head and looked at him with red, swollen eyes.

"What do you mean?"

"Well, it looks like you're going to be working here for a while," Clay said. "You picked up running the cash register pretty quick. And tonight, I'll show you how to make the register tape match up with the cash in your drawer. In the meantime, you need a pair of shoes."

He held out the twenty to her.

"You think twenty dollars will buy me a pair of shoes? I've bought socks that have cost twice as much."

"A pair of sneakers from the drugstore two blocks down. You'll get change back—think of it as a present from me."

She reluctantly took the bill.

"You also need a place to stay," Clay said more gently. "I take it you struck out on the hospitality search."

Jewell closed her eyes, willing back the tears that she had sworn were all gone.

"You can stay with me," Clay said. "I know it's not much, but you don't have many options."

"This has been the worst three days of my life," Jewell said.

"Darlin', welcome to the real world," Clay said. "There are folks who have days this bad all the time."

"So what do they do?"

"They get up and keep trying. And when they get beat down, they get back up again. You can do it yourself. If you managed to run this register for three hours, even with all your carrying on, you do know what it means to survive."

"Really?" She looked up at him.

"Really," he said, and brushed past her to pull the register tape for the day. Even now, her scent was decorative, floral, expensive. Women of her class didn't sweat no matter how hot and humid the day.

Self-reliance and determination to succeed, to thrive, were the traits he admired most. She was a delicate flower, and he didn't know whether she could survive or not. But telling her a little white lie wasn't a sin as far as Clay could tell.

Only thing he was worried about was when he would have to send her on her way. He was betting that, however much she tried to break her father's will, she would be leaving him for another destination, perhaps up north where the jobs were, perhaps to another man's bed here in town. Somehow, he thought saying goodbye to her might turn out to be as hard as when he'd nursed Samson and Delilah back to health. Thank God those dogs had simply refused to get out of the truck when he had taken them to the animal shelter.

He turned away from counting the cash to look at her as she picked out a Coke from the vending machine.

Her hairdresser, her manicurist, whoever did her clothes, would have a heart attack if they saw her now. Her skirt hem was ripped, her shoes were without their heels, her platinum hair fell about her shoulders in disobedient waves and the brilliant fuchsia polish on her nails was chipped and peeling. Clay smiled covertly as he realized a secret—the princess bit her nails.

He could bed her—he could do it now because she was weak and weary and a man could take advantage of that. But he wouldn't. And not just because he wanted to think of himself as a gentleman—not the gentleman defined by her monied class, but the gentleman of literature, the gentleman of the books he read and admired.

No, he wouldn't bed her because he didn't want a woman who would cling, who would suck every bit of strength from him and then fling him away when her fortunes changed. And that, Clay realized, was what she would do.

She would cling to him as surely as a drowning woman would cling to a lifesaver—until she got her money back.

Besides, he told himself, Jewell was probably the sort of woman who thought her mere appearance between the sheets was worthy of a man's gratitude. He liked a woman who made love to him with as much enthusiasm as he gave.

"Perhaps we should have some dinner?" she asked. "I'm exhausted and I'd love to put my feet up."

"Can't," Clay said abruptly, gathering up cash, register tape and receipts. "We've got work to do."

"Work? It's seven o'clock at night. I thought you said we were closed."

"There're three other gas stations. We've got to meet with their managers, pick up the cash, stop at the bank and then I have to reconcile what's going on in the cash register with the day's take."

"How long will all that take?"

Clay shrugged. "Coupla hours. I thought we'd stop and get your shoes on the way."

"I need more than shoes."

Clay shook his head. "No, you don't."

He pulled out a plastic-wrapped box from a locker beside the cash register. He shoved it across the counter toward her. She opened it as if it were a box of hissing water moccasins.

"How beautiful," she said dryly. "I presume it's silk."

"Cotton," Clay said. "Maybe from your daddy's own fields."

She pulled out the white overalls, sized small, groaning as she noticed the Smith's Gas Station embroidered in firehouse red thread on the back.

She checked the blue oval name patch above the right breast pocket.

"We can get you your own patch with your name," Clay assured. "The first guy who wore those was named Bill, and we've never kept anybody long enough to warrant changing the name."

"I don't intend to be here long enough to make it worth your while," she said grimly.

"Fine," he said. "Why don't you run upstairs and change?"

"Why don't I just stay here at the apartment for now? You go on ahead and do the cash-register stuff," she said, with persuasive, honeylike charm. "I've had a terribly, terribly long day."

"Do what you want." He shrugged, refusing to let her see that it made any difference to him what she did. "But let me tell you this—you've worked a total of three hours today. Most people work eight or nine. Lots of people work even more, with bosses asking for overtime. And then most folks go home and they have a second job—taking care of their family, tending to their house, running errands. Making your own way in the world is a hard thing. You can either learn that now or you can gamble that you're going to get your money back and never have to worry about this stuff again. Up to you. I'm going to wash up and then I'll be on my way."

He shoved past her to the stairs, taking them two at a time, hoping to burn off the crushed childish anticipation. He had wanted her company—he wasn't sure why, since all she'd probably do is complain or talk about her damned money.

Upstairs, he yanked off his shirt, lobbed it toward the laundry hamper next to the bathroom and missed for the first time in months. He scrubbed his hands furiously, until his nails gleamed alabaster and his calluses were red and raw. He was only slightly less brutal with his face, deciding impulsively to shave his five-o'clock shadow. Then he combed back his hair, puzzling again at which side of his family had given him an unruly cowlick. Then he opened the door to the bathroom, surprised to see the apartment was empty.

Princess must have decided to go out for a manicure, he decided.

He tugged a clean shirt from the armoire and trotted downstairs as he buttoned up. When he reached the final step, he glanced up and saw her leaning against the truck. He started to tuck his shirt into his jeans, and then felt the bulging manhood. It'd be better to leave the shirt out this evening, he thought.

"Wow," he said quietly as he walked up to her, putting one hand against the door of the truck, looking down at her with appraising eyes.

Though she had no doubt received thousands of compliments from hundreds of men, she seemed flustered by the single word, even more flustered than he was at the sight of her.

The coveralls, brilliant white cotton, covered her body with a paradoxical modesty that was more suggestive than a string bikini. The collar dipped low on her swelling breasts, and the waist nipped in tightly to exaggerate their fullness. And then, just when a man's eyes got used to the dangerous curves on top, his eyes were drawn to the fabric's strain at her hips.

His own hips were a trouble spot—his jeans, as forgiving as only well-worn ones can be, weren't big enough for Clay and his excitement.

And to think that all that lay between him and her was her coverall's zipper, which traveled from the inviting swell of her breasts down to the juncture of her legs.

Just a single pull . . .

It had been too long since he had had a woman. Too long since he had thought of pleasure. Too long since he had given himself permission to be a man and to feel the things that a man feels. And not because he had lacked for invitations.

No, it had been work that had become his mistress. A very hard mistress. For a year. A long year.

But there was a difference—now it was work for himself, for the first time in his life not tied to the responsibility of caring for others. Everyone taken care of. Now it was his turn, and he had driven himself more furiously than he had thought possible. When it had been supporting his mother and putting food into the mouths of his brothers and sisters, he had thought he was pushed to the limit.

Now, he realized, his limit had only just been met.

From beneath eyelids that drooped not from exhaustion but from desire, he gazed into her lilac-colored eyes.

And met her superior, smirking stare—he felt as if he had been slapped.

She knew what she did to him—she enjoyed what she did to him—and whatever grudging admiration he had given her during the day shriveled and died.

She smiled at him, a cool smile, one that communicated, *Look at me, admire me, desire me, but that is all, because no matter how debased I am at this moment, I am still too good for you.*

Two mischievous dimples appeared teasingly at either cheek, and her eyes sparkled with sunlight and superiority, between an inviting blue and a cold violet.

Her sexual nature had not been fully awakened—indeed, she was like a ripe, near-to-bursting fruit that would spoil if it were not soon plucked, if she were not soon taken by a man. It was clear she had been raised for pleasure, her own pleasure—though that pleasure seemed so far confined to shopping trips and parties and fine dining.

He raised his hands to grip her waist and felt his thigh twitch with anticipation—how ready it was to force her legs to part, to claim the right to guide her into territory she had not known and that would make her belong to him, belong in a way she would never belong to another man, belong in a way that no amount of diamonds set by Tiffany could ensure.

## Chapter Five

Jewell jutted her chin out, and a mischievous dimple twinkled at each cheek. Out of the corner of her eye, she noticed his hands clench and unclench and she felt a flicker of unfamiliar panic, wondering if—without wealth and social constraints—her smile no longer guaranteed her safety. As it had when there was money and position to back her up.

His espresso-colored eyes bore into hers, refusing to look away, refusing to defer. For one untamed moment, she reveled in his independence, his strength, his living outside the genteel rules of the society she had known.

With him, there would be no kisses on the air above her hand, no hackneyed compliments, no tentative caresses.

When he wanted her, he would take her, Jewell acknowledged to herself.

If he wanted her.

She was the first to look away, an act of submission she rued but could not prevent. It was an unfamiliar feeling, although she had so often unconsciously demanded a similar submission from every suitor she had ever known.

This was sexual submission, though without a single touch. Yet it inflamed her and enlivened her when she would have expected to feel only humiliation and shame. He undressed and appraised and measured her sexual value with his eyes. Only with his eyes.

Shocked, she realized she wanted his touch, wanted his roughened hands to touch her sleek skin, wanted his experienced flesh to master her own. She imagined giving herself to him right there against the truck—his hands guiding her buttocks, his mouth quenching her, his manhood thrusting into her until she found release.

But of course, all this would not be proper. Would not be ladylike. Would cause so many complications when it came time to tell Clay DeVries that she was returning to Pontchartreaux and he was staying behind. And most of all, she knew it was risky to take a "walk on the wild side" with Clay while her own position in the world was so tenuous.

Besides, her sexual impulses could not reverse twenty-eight years of training in the art of being a lady. That training—precise and allowing only the smallest range of disdainful responses to any overture—now took over, and she fixed on her lips a tight frown of dismissal.

That precise frown had been part of the proper Southern belle's repertoire for hundreds of years.

And it was still just as effective.

Clay slammed his fist against the hood of the truck with such force that a dent was left in his wake.

"Get in," he demanded.

She obeyed quickly, without a bantering reply. Yet as she took a deep breath and smoothed the imaginary wrinkles on the legs of her coveralls, she felt her confidence, her assuredness, return.

Almost a smile on her lips.

Which she quickly squelched as he slid into the driver's side of the truck.

"We have to set some ground rules about living together," he said huskily, pulling on aviator sunglasses.

"I couldn't agree more," Jewell said pleasantly. "You have to stop bossing me around."

*Bossing around* wasn't quite the phrase she was looking for, but telling him that he needed to stop making her feel like a wanton was a little harder to put into words.

Especially since he hadn't touched her, hadn't really done anything, had just looked at her with particular sexual hunger.

"Jewell, when you're working at the gas station, I am your boss so get used to it. The problem we have is after hours. Haven't you ever lived with anybody before?"

"No, I haven't, as a matter of fact. Have you?"

"Nobody recent," he said gruffly. "And not for very long. But I grew up with a full house."

Jewell hid her curiosity, her desire to know more about a woman who would share his bed. Was she beautiful? Had he loved her? Was there more than one?

She studied him and knew there must have been more than one.

And knew that each of them—rich or poor, young or old, experienced or naive—had come to him eagerly.

As eagerly as she would if her very survival didn't depend upon her resisting him. She had to get her birthright back and, when she did, she couldn't let the taint of their affair spoil her reentry into society.

Of course, Clay wasn't even thinking along these lines.

"There's nuts and bolts of being in the same household," Clay said. "Like sharing a bathroom and how to stay out of each other's way."

"Speaking of sharing a bathroom, I think yours is a pigsty. It's not so much that it's dirty, but it sure is messy."

"There's a reason for that. You've used up all five bath towels I own, and every last one of them you leave on the floor as if you expect a maid to pick them up. And how come you never put the lid back on anything—whether it's shampoo, toothpaste or talc? My bathroom was doing just fine until you went through it like a tornado."

Jewell thought back. "All right, I'm sorry," she said. "I guess I've always had Mia to pick up after me."

"Who?"

"Mia, our housekeeper. She's been with the family for years. She spoils me."

"Tell me anybody who hasn't."

He stared at her—but with his glasses, Jewell couldn't see his eyes, couldn't measure whether there was sympathy or disgust at play.

"Tell me something," he continued. "I'm curious. How much did your father leave this Mia?"

"Five hundred dollars."

"How old is she?"

"In her sixties, I think. She was hired by my grandfather. Even when the Whittingtons didn't have a penny, they had Mia."

"And all your father left her was five hundred?"

"Hey, wait a minute! You have no concern for me, but you're worried about Mia?"

"You've got your whole life ahead of you. She's not going to get another job."

"You're probably right about that. But she's staying on until Michael sells the house."

"So your father left her without a pension?"

"I feel very bad about that, but it's true. My father had already given her the carriage house that she lives in—maybe he expected her to sell it and live off the proceeds. Live where, I don't know. She's been in the carriage house since before I was born."

"Doesn't that make you suspicious? That he didn't provide for Mia? That she's going to have to move out of the carriage house?"

Jewell felt a righteous anger well up inside of her.

"Clay, I've thought right from the start the will was suspicious. But every time I say so, people think I'm just a spoiled brat who wants to take food out of the mouths of homeless people. You, especially."

"Did you read this thing?" he asked, starting the engine of the truck.

"The will? No."

"You should go down to the courthouse or back to that fool lawyer and demand a copy."

"So you believe me? That something's fishy about this will?"

"I'm conceding only that maybe something's wrong."

While a day or two ago, she would have been satisfied only with a concession that she had been robbed, today she was just happy that somebody was doubting, that somebody might be persuaded that she was right.

And some part of her sensed that having Clay on her side meant a lot. He was a man with such internal strengths that she knew he was a powerful ally.

"I promise you, Clay," she said impulsively. "When I get my money back, when I'm back at Pontchartreaux, I'm not going to forget you."

The words died on her lips when she saw his face darken and then freeze with a sardonic smile.

"Actually, Princess, I hope you do forget me," he said grimly. "Better that way."

Her throat clutched, but she said nothing.

They didn't exchange another word until they reached Achtacatchez and the first gas station for which they would do the books.

"I CAN'T WAIT to get home," Jewell sighed as she slipped off her sneakers. She settled into the bench seat of the truck. "I'm going to make a nice plate of plain pasta, just a little lemon and butter on the side. Maybe some black pepper. I'm going to take a hot, hot, hot bath. And we have to stop at the drugstore for nail glue, because I broke another one of my tips pulling the register tape out at the second station you took me to. Hey, wait a minute, what's this place?"

Clay squeezed the truck into a patch of flattened kudzu between two other pickups. He killed the engine and nodded at the two-story frame house that wouldn't have been worth notice except for the chanky-chank music and high-pitched laughter coming from it.

And for the twenty-foot-tall sign with Al's Roadhouse scrawled in brilliant red neon.

"This, darling, is where my kind hangs out," Clay said.

"No way." Jewell shook her head.

"Yes way. A man can't get by on plain pasta, a little lemon and butter on the side. Even with black pepper. And I still don't know what I had for dinner last night, since everything at L'Hermitage was under a sauce or topped with a pastry shell."

"But why here? This looks so. . ."

"Think of it as a cultural experience. They drink beer right from the bottle and eat chicken-fried steak for an appetizer. And the music is pure country—no string quartets."

"I thought you were the one who was so tired."

"Man's gotta eat. Man's gotta have a beer."

"Why this place?"

"It's my younger brother's. I'm always assured of a free meal. And he never charges me for beer, either."

"Your younger brother owns his own business?"

"Yeah, you got a problem with that?"

"No, I'm just glad to hear that he's really made something of himself."

"And I haven't?"

"I didn't mean it like that."

"It's all right," he said amiably. "While you're comparing what a great success he is to what a failure I am, add into your calculations that I'm a free-loader, too. Every night, if I can. It's on the way home from the bank. Most nights, I stop off at the deposit window, drop off the cash for the evening and head for Al's. I never pay for a meal if I don't have to. Ever since the Pretty Good Café went out of business."

He didn't mention the previous evening, but he knew she was thinking of L'Hermitage. And thinking that she had paid for dinner.

Aw, let her think what she wants, he thought to himself. Probably easier for her if she thought he was nothing.

"Clay, I don't care if you don't like to pay for dinner. I want to go home," Jewell said plaintively. Funny how that one-room apartment on top of the station was already home, she thought. "I've had a long day, a day where all I want to do is curl up in a ball and hope lightning doesn't strike me again."

"You've had three days in a row like that," Clay conceded. "But you've tried hot baths and hiding your head. Maybe this place'll change your luck. Come on. Al will feed you, too."

"Glad to know I'm such a cheap date."

"Actually, I think you're pretty expensive, given what I'm getting in return from you."

Leaving Jewell to sputter her indignation, he strode toward the house. A laughing, embracing couple tumbled out onto the porch. They gave Clay a cheery greeting, and Clay quietly responded.

She felt trapped as she angrily yanked at the laces on her sneakers. Go into a roadhouse? Drink beer out of bottles and eat food that was slow death for your arteries and high in calories, too? Be seen on the arm of Clay DeVries, gas-station attendant? As if she would let him touch her.

As Jewell swiped on some **lip**stick and gave up on her hair, she scanned the weeds, grass and gravel that served as parking lot. The pickup trucks, late-model boats-for-cars, and the motorcycles reassured her that nobody she knew would be inside.

Oh, the arrogance of him, she thought as she slid out of the pickup and touched her tired feet to the ground. To think she had to be here when she could be in bed asleep. To think she had to be here with him when she could be . . . what?

"You know I don't want to be here," she growled at him as he took her elbow and introduced her to his friends on the porch.

A giggly woman and a proud, silent man smiled at her.

"Darlin', you can leave anytime you want," Clay whispered back.

And then Jewell realized her defeat.

Nobody except Clay would have her. Mindy would always be "unavailable." Ditto for Arianna and Genie and even Winfield's sister. While it was funny in a way to make each housekeeper squirm for new excuses as to why her mistress couldn't come to the phone, Jewell promised herself no more phone calls, no more humiliation.

That meant she had no place to go, nobody to be with.

And she knew that she shouldn't, couldn't, blame Clay for that.

But, of course, she did.

"Jewell Whittington, I know you," the woman before her squealed. "I've done your house for parties."

"Huh?" Jewell had never seen this woman before in her life.

"Mia's hired me to serve appetizers and drinks at your house for years. I've celebrated New Year's Eve at your house for the past ten." Then she caught herself, remembering that she was talking to Jewell Whittington, princess of the Pontchartreaux estate.

Jewell was suddenly aware of how artificially people had always acted around her.

"I've got two young ones, and the extra money has always helped out at Christmas," the woman added, now babbling embarrassingly. "Roger here's worked at your house, too. The electrical work on the guest house last summer paid for a down payment on our car."

Roger thought to shake hands with Jewell, but then, as he wiped his hands against his jeans, reconsidered. His hands were not good enough to touch hers, he seemed to acknowledge. And Jewell felt his shame and wondered why she had never noticed how people acted around her before.

Her house had moved and worked as if by magic, and to acknowledge that people, living and breathing people, were responsible for the things she had taken so much for granted, was painful.

She now smiled with as much graciousness as she could muster. But that graciousness was the kind of royalty and rulers and didn't put anyone at ease.

"I'm sorry to hear about the death of your father," Roger said.

"Thank you," Jewell said stiffly. She supposed, from Roger's wife's stare, that she sounded cold and superior.

Then, silence. Or nearly so, since the raucous music seemed to come from a distance, and the laughter and good cheer from inside were muted.

Jewell felt the question linger in the air as the couple looked over her gas-station coveralls and then zeroed in on Clay's hand at her arm.

What was she doing here?

Why was she slumming with Clay?

Why couldn't she get what she wanted from him in the privacy of bed and go back to her world and leave them to theirs?

"Well, Clay, it's been nice to run into you," Roger said, breaking the silence. He tugged on his wife's arm. "We gotta run. The baby-sitter will have a tizzy fit if we're late. But it's our anniversary, so we had to celebrate."

Jewell suffered through the goodbyes and the curious stares, and a single thought ran through her head. How awful that this roadhouse would be the only place a couple could afford to celebrate their marriage. She resolved that when she got her money back, the first thing she would do would be to write a hefty check to them and tell them to go to L'Hermitage for a nice treat.

The idea surprised her.

She was not normally a generous person with her money—abiding by her father's rules of never loaning money to a friend and only making charitable contributions to institutions with IRS tax-deductible status.

"What were their names?" she asked Clay.

"Roger and Mary Duncan," Clay said. "Why? You thinkin' of inviting them to tea at Pontchartreaux?"

She shook her head. "I'm thinking of sending them a little anniversary check when I get my house back."

"Make it big. They work hard, and it's tough getting by—especially with triplets."

"Triplets?"

"Four years old. It was a bit of a surprise at the time."

"I'll send them three thousand dollars. One for each child."

"They'd appreciate it."

She followed Clay into the house, squeezing past the boisterous crowd to a long plank bar. A five-piece band was set up in front of what would have been, in the house's previous incarnation, the living-room fireplace. There was no definable dance floor, but couples swayed together, clapped their hands, embraced and sang to each other the familiar refrains in every corner, on the staircase, at their tables covered with blue gingham and at the bar. Weaving through the crowd, waitresses hoisted trays with dozens of beer bottles and platters of steaks and fried chicken.

Several men tipped their hat in Clay's direction, a few clapped him on the shoulder as he squeezed Jewell toward the bar and two women attempted to pull him into an embrace but thought better of it when they noticed Jewell on his arm. She attracted some stares— mostly curiosity, but some hostility mixed in.

She was an intruder and she knew it.

"Hey, bro," the bartender greeted them as they found two empty stools near the wall. He laid two Dixie longnecks and a bowl of chips in front of them. "Who's your beautiful friend?"

"Jewell Whittington," Clay said, grabbing a bottle and offering the other to Jewell. "Jewell, this is Al. Al, you know Jewell. By reputation if not personally."

Al looked like Clay—although maybe not quite as tall and spread a little more thickly in the middle. But the eyes were the same, though a fern green instead of brown. And he wore glasses, small wire frames that he pushed back on his nose. He looked at Jewell with undisguised curiosity.

"Jewell? Jewell Whittington? Of the Whittingtons on Pontchartreaux?" He shoved his glasses firmly onto the bridge of his nose and stared at her. "Evenin' ma'am."

"You can call me Jewell."

"Yes, ma'am. I mean, sure, Jewell," Al sputtered, and looked at his brother. "You're taking her out?"

"It's not a date," Clay said. "She just started working at Smith's."

Al's jaw dropped, and he abandoned any pretense of believing his brother.

"Works at Smith's?" He squinted at the name stitched on the breast pocket of her coveralls.

"Says Bill, but we're changing that," Clay explained.

"You got it bad, brother," Al said, shaking his head. "You always did, and I gotta admit that every time you've set your sights on a goal, you've worked like a demon and gotten what you wanted. I guess that includes you, apparently, Miss Whittington."

"Jewell."

"Right. Jewell."

"He hasn't 'gotten' me," she said. Being well-bred, her voice carried just enough of her indignation so that there was no doubt in Al's mind that he had overstepped an invisible boundary of good taste and courtesy.

"Yes, ma'am. I mean, Miss Jewell. Uh, Jewell."

"I told her that you were the best cook on the delta," Clay said, not noticing how much sweat beaded up on his brother's forehead or how Al's eyes skittered back and forth behind his thick glasses. "I told her I tried to get here every night of the week."

"You sure do," Al agreed, grateful to his brother for steering the conversation away from his faux pas. "He eats my food, drinks my beer, snaps his fingers to my music and dances with my waitresses. And I ain't never seen fit to give him a check. By the way, where were you last night?"

"L'Hermitage," Clay said.

Al whistled. "I hear their food's okay, but I think we got better fried chicken. And much better atmosphere," he said, pausing to look first at Clay and then at Jewell. He opened his mouth, ready to inquire even more, and then shut it again.

"Keep out of it, brother," Clay said softly.

The two brothers seemed to have an understanding, because Al simply shook his head and shoved his glasses back into place.

"So what'll it be tonight?" he asked.

"Why don't you give me some of that chicken?" Clay decided. "What about you, Jewell?"

"I don't know, I'd have to see a menu."

"Al doesn't have menus, Jewell. This isn't that kind of place. There's fried chicken, chicken-fried steak, and more fried chicken. Go with the chicken."

"Coming right up," Al said, without waiting for Jewell's assent. He slipped back into the kitchen.

Clay clanked his beer against hers and took a long pull.

"So what do you think of this place?" he asked as proudly as if he owned it himself.

They turned together, his shoulder brushing against hers, to survey the bar, the customers at their tables, the dancers swaying to and fro.

"It's seems pretty nice," Jewell admitted. "Everyone looks like they're having a good time."

"That's Al's gift," Clay said, pointing out his brother, who had come back from the kitchen and was greeting people at their tables. "Making people comfortable, making people feel like their money is well spent, like they're not just going out to eat, they're celebrating something. Every time they walk in the door. I tell you, Jewell, this place of his is only two years old, but one day it'll be the most famous club in all the Mississippi."

"He's ambitious," Jewell said with just the slightest hint of reproach.

"Oh, and you think I'm not."

"I didn't say that."

"You didn't have to."

"I think ambition is a very good trait in a man," she said neutrally.

"You think ambition is the most important trait in a man. If I had a little more of it, you'd be more inclined to like me, might even want to bed me. But as long as I'm just a no-'count mechanic, you look down on me. And a woman can't stand a man she looks down on."

Jewell flushed. "I didn't say any of that."

"You didn't have to," he said. "But I want you to know that I live by my own rules and, under those rules, I'm as successful as your father or your fiancé or any number of other men in your class."

"And just what are your rules?"

"Stand by your family," he said. "Take care of the weak. Give an honest day's work for an honest day's wage. Very different from the 'greed is good' you've been raised on, wouldn't you say?"

"I think you're a very pompous man," Jewell said icily.

Clay threw back his head and laughed.

"You're absolutely right. What I just said did sound a little preachy, didn't it?"

"Yeah," she agreed, laughing with him.

Their eyes met, and some spark of understanding passed between them, something that made them realize they were two of a kind. Survivors, even if one of them hadn't had her mettle tested yet. Survivors of a very special sort, the ones who can face adversity and troubles without losing their essential good nature, without losing their laughter and their joy.

The connection between them was sudden and needed no words, no clinking of their beers in celebratory toast, no shaking of hands. They just had to look at each other in recognition.

"Ah, Jewell, you have such a beautiful smile," Clay said. "Come on, dance with me. Pretend for just a moment that we're friends."

He pulled her from the bar onto the small crescent of floor space in front of the band. He put his arms around her waist just as the band began a slow, moody Texas-style waltz.

Jewell wanted to give in to the moment, to feel the pleasure, to hear the music and let herself be caressed by a handsome, sexy man.

She could only do this if she set aside the Jewell Whittington of old, the one who was—she confessed truthfully—prissy, coolly polite, spoiled and pampered.

But if there wasn't anything left of the Jewell of old, what was there?

A twenty-eight-year-old woman without a penny to her name.

Without a family.

Without a home.

She looked up into Clay's sable brown eyes. They challenged her to protest as he pressed his hips against hers—tentatively at first and then, when she gave him no resistance, with increasing pressure. Though the band was loud, she could hear more clearly than music his ragged breath.

Between them lay nothing but their own fears.

"I think it would be a mistake..." he began.

"I think it would be a mistake, too," she said at the same moment.

"We're both pretty certain we're about to screw up," he said. "Let's see if we agree about what will be our downfall. What do you think would be a mistake?''

''To have sex. It would...complicate things. I have my life to go back to. You have...yours.''

''You're too polite to say what you mean, that I really don't have a life.'' He sighed, and lifted his head and held hers to him. She could feel the deep, quickened pulse at the base of his throat. ''Princess, I'll help you get back to your castle. Maybe it's where you really belong. And maybe it'd be better for me, too, because I never was the kind of kid who liked to press his nose against the window of stores he couldn't afford just for the chance to see the toys.''

She jerked away from him. ''You'll help me prove my claim to my father's money?'' she demanded excitedly.

''Yeah,'' he said, reluctantly nodding. ''We'll go down to the courthouse tomorrow, or maybe we should go back to the lawyer. Whatever it takes. Something might be in the will, something might not be. But I promise you that whatever it takes, I'll be there to help. I'll see it through until you're back where you belong.''

''Oh, Clay, that's wonderful!'' she exclaimed. ''At last, I feel like I have an ally, a real friend.''

She hugged him exuberantly, without holding back. For a moment, the briefest moment, Clay let himself believe it was him that she adored, him that she trusted, him that she loved.

And then, the moment of delusion over, he pulled her arms from around his neck and smiled ruefully.

''Jewell, I meant every word I said. About family. About helping. About working hard. That's what a

man is in the end. His word. His beliefs. Nothing
more.''

But his words were lost to her—the band had struck
up a raucous version of ''Watch Me Walk Out That
Door,'' and the crowd surged onto the tiny dance floor
for line dancing. He and Jewell were quickly taken up
by other dancers. He found himself in the arms of a
woman who had been eyeing him for half an hour.
Jewell was twirling in the embrace of a friend of his.
He briefly looked to Jewell, wondering if she would
turn up her nose because this wasn't the cotillion.

But she had thrown back her head with delight, her
blond hair loose and flowing, her teeth gleaming as she
laughed with pleasure.

JEWELL FLUNG HERSELF onto the bed.

''Come on up here!'' she called out. ''Come on, it's
all right. I'm not going to bite.''

Samson and Delilah hesitantly approached the bed,
looked at each other for confirmation of the invitation they had just received and leapt up into the bed
and settled onto the pillows around Jewell's head.

''You, too,'' she called out to Clay, who hung back
at the door, ostensibly looking through the mail. ''I've
had a wonderful evening. The best. This isn't a se-
duction. I just want you to be comfortable for a moment. That couch is awful.''

Clay smiled as he lay next to her, on his stomach,
careful not to touch her. The bed was as divided as if
there had been a fence put up the middle of the mattress—Samson and Delilah, he mused, guardians of
the princess's virtue.

"Was it really the best?" he asked. "I mean, there wasn't any champagne, there wasn't an orchestra, nobody fancy did the flowers."

"But we had the best fried chicken in all of Mississippi," Jewell replied tartly. "And the best dancing in all the world. My feet hurt so much."

She flipped off her sneakers, letting them topple to the floor. She was just a little bit tipsy, the two beers taking their toll on a tired and worn body.

"Was it really the best?" Clay teased again.

"Oh, it was! Better than the Governor's Ball, better than the Magnolia Dance, better than anybody's coming out. Oh, Clay, it was a wonderful night. And you know, you're really my friend. Maybe the only real friend I have. I mean, you don't care if I'm wealthy or not, you just care about... Oh, God, Clay, you don't like me, do you?"

"Me? No, I mean yes. I like you. Sure. I mean that isn't what I was thinking at all."

"It's okay if you don't like me. I'm beginning to believe I might not be very likable. I'm stubborn and spoiled and think money is the only thing that matters."

"Maybe you are those things, just a little. But I still like you."

"You do?"

"Yeah. It used to be just lust," he said. "Oh, no, don't worry, I'm not going to seduce you. It's just I admired you from afar—this was years ago—I wanted to bed you, but boy, were you the bossiest, spoiled-est girl I ever met."

"How did you know?"

"One day during August, hottest day of the summer, must have been ten years ago, you wanted azaleas to line the courtyard. You were giving a party for hundreds of your closest friends. Do you remember what happened?"

She looked at him blankly. There had been so many parties and so many different decisions with each one. Flowers, wines, which silver to use...

"Uh-oh," she said. "Now I remember."

"We planted five hundred azaleas. Pink azaleas. Took me and five other gardeners a whole day."

"Don't remind me what happened next. I was such a jerk."

"You wanted white."

"Was it really that important to me?"

"It was important enough for you to demand that we uproot all five hundred blooms and replant in white."

"You must have thought I was being a little exacting."

"I thought a lot worse," Clay said amiably. "And so did everyone else on the crew."

They laughed.

"And now?" Jewell asked, suddenly serious.

"Now I think everything you were was simply a product of what you had been raised with," Clay said. "Your father was the one who gave you the power to do crazy things like that. But you have to choose now. Choose what kind of person you're going to be for the rest of your life."

She looked up at the ceiling and sighed. "I don't know what kind of person I am without the Whittington money," she confessed.

"You're a great dancer," Clay said. "And you picked up working a cash register pretty quickly. And you talk like you're going to be more generous toward people like Roger and Mary, who could use a helping hand. And I bet you're a real good...kisser."

He stared at her as if he were surprised by his own words. Surprised as she was. The dogs were startled from their comfortable sleep and jumped off the bed.

"I better not," Clay said. "I've wanted to since I was a laborer in your garden and you used to sunbathe on the courtyard in a skimpy bikini. You never even noticed me. Never noticed any of the crew. We could have been invisible. Nineteen years old and I knew I wanted to kiss you—didn't take me long to figure out what else I'd want to do after I kissed you enough times. I've never quite gotten you out of my system. I better quit talking. Once I start, Jewell, I warn you, I'm not going to be able to stop."

"Would I want you to?"

"Yeah, you'd want me to stop. But you might not want me to stop until tomorrow morning. It's a mistake, Jewell, just like you said. Because when you want to run back to the castle, you won't want to remember that my roughened hands have touched you."

He stood up and pulled off his shirt, revealing the tough, muscular chest. She thought he would take her then, and some part of her hoped he would. That he would take responsibility for deciding, that she could simply surrender to the pleasure, without second-guessing herself about whether it was right or wrong, mistake or not.

"We gotta make some rules, even if you're staying for just a few days," he said, throwing his shirt into a hamper by the door to the bathroom. "One of us has to sleep in the bed, and the other person has to not sleep in the bed. It isn't going to work any other way."

She gulped down her feelings—what?—could it be disappointment? "Do you want the bed?"

"Nah, you take it tonight. I had it last night and I'll take it tomorrow. I can sleep on the couch."

He pulled a thick volume from the bookshelf. "Just want to do a little bit of reading before I go to sleep," he explained before sprawling on the sofa. The dogs gravitated to him and curled themselves around his body.

Jewell took a T-shirt from the armoire and went to the bathroom to change out of her coveralls. After brushing her teeth and hair—bemoaning the dark roots that were just starting to show—she washed her face and hands, amazed at the unseen dirt that blackened the water. Two silk tips were chipped, and she reluctantly peeled them off, vowing she'd get supplies for a touch-up manicure the next day.

No way were her standards completely out the window.

Then she rinsed out the Valentino ecru lace bra and panties and hung them over the shower-curtain rod to dry. She slipped on the dry undies from the night before and pulled on a T-shirt, stretching the cotton down over her silk panties.

When she opened the door to the rest of the apartment, he looked up only once. With enough critical regard that she turned around, picked up the towel she had discarded on the floor and put it carefully in the hamper.

Then she walked to the bed, certain he would look up. After all, how interesting could *Recapturing the Constitution: Analysis and Text* be? But his eyes never roamed from the page as she walked by, even though at her every footstep the shirt hinted at the floral silk and creamy skin beneath.

She slipped under the sheets.

"Well, good night," she said, feeling oddly bereft.

"Good night," Clay said, turning the page.

She put her head down on the pillow and closed her eyes.

She counted to one hundred.

She listed as many state capitals as she could remember.

She listed the kings and queens of the English succession beginning with King John I and working her way up to Elizabeth II. Well, as best as she could remember.

And all with her eyes closed.

He slapped his book shut. The dogs yelped and scurried to the safety of the bed. Still, Jewell's eyes remained shut. She could feel his eyes upon her, smell his clean scent of lime and musk and hear his breathing as he stood so near the bed.

"This isn't going to work if you act like a tease," he said softly. "And this isn't going to work if I act like an animal."

A second later, the door slammed and she heard his steps disappear into the night. She raced to the window in time to see him straddle a motorcycle parked at the very edge of the garage. He revved up the engine and drove out into the earliest, darkest morning.

She turned around to the empty apartment. Two dogs panting at the foot of the bed. She had never been lonely when she slept alone before.

"I'm not a tease," she indignantly told the dogs.

No, she was just a woman at war with herself—her body moving her in one direction, while her mind furiously applied the brakes. It would be a mistake, a terrible mistake, to use him and then try to cast him aside. She was certain he wouldn't make it easy for her.

He would complicate things.

"But, oh, what a treat it would be," she said, flopping down on the bed and letting the dogs cuddle near her.

An hour later, she managed to drift into sleep, and as she shifted and turned in a dreamless sleep, one part of her was listening for the roar of the motorcycle and the clatter of his keys at the door.

## Chapter Six

"What horrible and disgusting thing are you doing now?" Clay asked, slipping into the office from the door to the garage.

He slam-dunked the paper towel he had used to wipe his hands into the trash bin behind Jewell.

"I'm peeling my silk tips off," Jewell said, not looking up from her task at the counter. "I broke off two nails yesterday and three this morning. Salvaging them is as hopeless as keeping kudzu weed from growing all over."

"And what is that smell?"

"It's the solvent that dissolves the glue that holds the silk tips in place."

"It's awful."

"I know. But we women go through a lot to look great. In my case, I'm going through a lot to end up with stubby, ugly fingernails. Kind of like good grooming in reverse."

Clay leaned across the counter, and Jewell resisted the urge to pull back from him. She had become more resolute that she would reject any sexual play between them.

That he wanted her—even as she was, tips broken, hair uncoiffed, dressed in ridiculous coveralls—she didn't doubt.

That she wanted him was a notion she chose not to examine too closely.

But actions would never follow on the heels of desire.

Because she knew that she wanted her life back—and she didn't want any complications getting in the way of returning to her home and to her world.

So, more determined than ever to avoid a sexual entanglement, she found herself paradoxically more aware of every volt of sexual current between them.

When he leaned toward her, she smelled his musk and heat.

She reopened the bottle of solvent and was hit in the face with the acrid odor.

So much for Clay and the seductive power of scent.

She peeled off the last silk nail of her left hand and threw it in the garbage.

"That looks like torture," he said.

"You're right. It sure doesn't feel great when I have to yank these tips. But I called my manicurist and found out that I've been paying forty dollars a week for upkeep on these things."

"Forty bucks a week? Do you know how much that is a year?"

"I've never really thought about it. Let's see…two thousand dollars?"

"Yeah. That's a lot of money to pay for somebody else's nails."

"They're not somebody else's. They're made out of silk."

"Silkworm webs. Still disgusting."

"Well, it doesn't matter, since I don't have the money anymore. I can't spend nearly a day's worth of pay every week on my nails. Soon as I get back home, of course, I'll go back to tips. I've had them for years."

Clay picked up her right hand and scrutinized it carefully. Long, thin, tapered fingers set off by fuchsia-colored talons. Jewell was surprised by the frisson of electricity between them in even such an innocent touch. She pulled back her hand, and then he looked up, studying her. She wondered if he knew the effect he had on her.

He knew she was afraid of him, afraid not of physical violence but of sex itself. He wondered how she had managed to get nearly to thirty with her innocence intact. Because there was innocence there—even if he knew there had been other men.

If you could call a worm like Winfield Sims IV a man, Clay thought grimly, deciding that if he ever got the chance he'd tell Winfield he was a wimp and a coward for losing Jewell when she needed him most.

But the funny thing was, Clay would bet his paychecks for a year that Winfield Sims IV would come calling the minute Jewell got her inheritance back.

He'd also bet that Jewell would sport Winfield's diamond and take those vows—and ten years from now Mr. and Mrs. Winfield Sims IV would joke about the days she spent "slumming" as a gas-station employee.

And Clay would be long forgotten.

Clay didn't say anything, but picked up her other hand, the one clear of polish and tips, nails cut to the very quick.

"I like this hand better," he said. "I like the fact that the fingers are clean and I like the white moon on the base of each nail. I also like the fact that they're short—I'd hate to have you leave scratch marks on my back."

She yanked her hand back from him as if his fingers were the jaws of a cottonmouth. The suggestion was unmistakable, and was accompanied by a grin somehow both boyishly sweet and predatory.

"Don't joke about that anymore," she ordered hotly.

"Don't joke about what anymore?" he asked, pulling a soda from the glass-enclosed refrigerator. "Hey, turnabout's fair play. You tease me all the time. You don't even have to open your mouth to do it half the time. You do it with your hair and your walk and your smile."

"I do not."

"You do, darlin'."

"I deeply resent the suggestion that—"

"I deeply resent that you can be the most suggestive woman I've ever seen just walking across the parking lot and then you can act like so indignant when we're face-to-face."

"I don't walk in a suggestive manner."

"You might not mean to, but you do."

"Your mind's in the gutter."

"That's what you'd expect, though, isn't it? Lower-class guy, got his brains between his legs."

"No, that's not it at all."

"Well, explain it to me sometime."

He sprawled on the orange vinyl couch normally reserved for customers. He closed his eyes, sighing deeply.

"Is this argument because you didn't get any sleep last night?" Jewell asked, adding with perfectly controlled innocence, "I didn't hear you come in."

"It took me a while to calm down last night," he conceded reluctantly. "Jewell, you can't believe what you do to me."

He opened his eyes and stared at her with naked need. The shadows beneath his coffee-colored eyes, the result of too much missed sleep, only made his gaze even more sexually suggestive.

It flashed through Jewell's mind for the first time that it was unfair of her to take his bed, to walk before him in near-complete undress, to live with him — all the while refusing his advances. In a perfect world, her single word — no — would close the sexual debate.

But it wasn't a perfect world. While never so crass as to force himself upon her or manipulate her into his bed, he wanted her, desired her, would take her in an instant if she said yes. That he would want her didn't intimidate her, didn't make her fear or loathe him, but it did fill her with a pride she had never known before, a feminine pride that is not displayed but cherished privately.

In this imperfect dance, she said no but knew she acted and felt so contrary. And he stilled his internal primitive man who would ignore complexities of emotion and take her.

"Maybe I should move out," she offered.

"You don't have anywhere to go."

"I could do it—I could go back to Memphis. Find a job. Get an apartment."

"First of all, I don't think you'd last two minutes on your own. And second, you wouldn't be here, where you need to be if you're going to get your father's money. Besides, Princess, this is only temporary. Very temporary. I can live with a few nights without sleep. Until you move back home. It's not you. It can't be. It's probably that couch. It's the most uncomfortable thing I've ever laid down on. Never noticed it when all it was used for was reading and having the guys over to watch a ball game."

"You take the bed tonight," Jewell offered graciously.

"I'm planning on it. In fact, I'm looking forward to it, more than you could ever imagine. But—wait a minute—that means you're not going to get any sleep tonight."

She shrugged, suggesting that she knew that was part of the deal, part of life.

"I guess I'm beginning to realize that I should be thankful just to have a dry and safe place to sleep. You know, I thought I could count on friends, on Winfield, on people who were associated with my family. I knew I couldn't count on my half brother, but I knew I could count on my father. Now I'm not sure I can count on anything, but I know I'm pretty lucky to have you as a friend. And you are a friend, aren't you?"

Clay looked at her, suddenly seeing the loneliness that she probably only now realized was a vital part of her life.

To call him a friend, a guy she'd never known existed two days ago.

To call him a friend, a guy who wasn't her kind at all.

"Yeah, friend," he said, an unexpected choke to his voice.

*Friend.* He rolled the word around his tongue and realized that the word had a way of emasculating a man, of closing off his possibilities.

"And I'm grateful for even the couch," Jewell offered.

He let one eyebrow arch suggestively. "Princess, did I just hear you say something that comes mighty close to 'thank you'?"

"Yeah, of course, don't I always say thank you? I haven't been raised in a barn. I know my manners."

"No, as a matter of fact, you don't always say thank you," Clay said. "But, I guess if we're really friends, you don't have to say it all the time. Once in a while is enough."

"All right, thank you for taking me in and helping me out."

"You're welcome," Clay said. "You know, maybe we can do something about this sleeping business. We can just have the dogs sleep in the middle of the bed. Between us. That way, your morals will stay intact, and maybe I can get some sleep. That's right. Samson and Delilah, the virtue police."

THAT AFTERNOON, he taught her how to pump the gas. Though the pumps were self-serve, Clay made it a practice to help many of the elderly customers who used self-serve to save money but weren't vigorous enough to do the pump work themselves. He taught her how to check the oil and how to pump air into tires. She taught herself how to use the squeegee to wash windows, though the first few times she ended up spraying windshield-wiper fluid on drivers who weren't quick enough to duck.

It was a busy day, and after he taught her what she needed to know to keep the place running, Clay disappeared into the garage, where he worked on the transmission of a late-model car. As the sun dipped lower and the clock ticked past three and then four o'clock, Jewell started to fidget.

At precisely four-thirty, he slammed shut the hood on the car he was working on, told her to call Mrs. Cohen and tell her the car would be waiting for her in the parking lot, then disappeared upstairs. Minutes later, he was cleaned up, shaved, dressed in a pressed oxford shirt and khaki pants.

He flipped the Open sign hung on the door.

"Ready to go?"

She nodded.

He threw her his keys. "Then you drive," he said. "I'm exhausted. We go first to the courthouse and then to the three stations to close out the cash registers."

"Then to Al's?"

"You wanna cook?"

"You don't own any pots or pans."

He stared at her. "We'll order pizza," he said. "Because I want to get back home early—we go to Al's, we'll be there all night. I swear I haven't gotten a wink of sleep since I met you. Glad you're driving."

"Uh, Clay," she said, dangling the keys in front of him, "I can't drive stick shift."

"Well, you better learn by five o'clock, 'cause that's when the courthouse closes."

"And you say you're too tired to drive?"

"Yeah, darling, way too tired to be trusted on the road."

He smiled then, with enough challenge in his twinkling eyes that she knew, knew to the very core of her being, that he had enough strength to drive for four days straight without closing his eyes. That he could cook any meal he wanted. That he could handle all the work at the station. That taking the time to teach her everything today had been more trouble than it was worth to him.

But for some reason, he demanded this from her, always demanded. More than anyone had ever done before, any had ever dared.

And she'd show him.

"Let's go," she said, grabbing her purse from the shelf underneath the register. He was already sitting in the passenger's seat of the pickup when she got in. She fumbled with the keys, looking for the ignition, before he smoothly took the keys from her and slipped one of them into the slit on the side of the steering wheel.

"How much time do we have?" she asked. Her watch, a twenty-five-hundred-dollar Cartier, was safely tucked in the medicine cabinet in the upstairs apartment.

"Twenty minutes and the courthouse is three miles away."

"We've got plenty of time, then."

"I hope you're right."

They got there with a bare minute to spare.

And along the way, Jewell learned to drive a pickup—lurching to unexpected stops, turning so widely that she nearly plowed into cars parked on the opposite side of the road, killing the engine in the middle of intersections. While some folks were in a hurry or just plain terrified out of their wits by her novice run, most people gave her a friendly wave or a thumbs-up gesture meant to be comforting. Maybe they saw how white her face got when she panicked.

Mostly, she thought they saw Clay in the passenger's seat—and the wave and friendly gestures wouldn't have come so quickly if he hadn't been noticed there. His reassuring smile told her and all the world that he trusted her with his truck—in this part of Mississippi, that sentiment was much more evidence of emotional closeness than the fact that he must trust her with his life, as well.

But by the time they hit midtown, Jewell felt confidence in her abilities, so much so that if there was a way to make a pickup swagger, she would have found it.

Still, they had to take the stairs two at a time, squeezing into the door to the county clerk's office with a flirtatious smile from Clay to the stern, white-haired keeper of the records.

They sat on the lawn outside the clematis-covered stone courthouse, sharing a Coke bought from the basement vending machine.

Jewell shook her head in disbelief once more as she slowly went through the pages of torturously phrased legal documents.

Bottom line was that she had nothing.

She was utterly defeated.

"It's not so bad, Jewell," Clay said, lying down and covering his eyes from the late-afternoon sun. "You're young, you've got a lot of education and you can start over. Although it sounds like he thought you were going to marry Winfield and have plenty of money with him so that Charles's money going to the homeless shelter wouldn't be so bad."

"But that didn't happen," Jewell argued. "We'd been engaged for two years and hadn't set a wedding date. Doesn't that tell you something?"

"Tells me you didn't want to marry him. If I were thinking of marrying, my engagement would last exactly twenty minutes."

"Twenty minutes?"

"That's how long it takes to get from my place to the courthouse. I don't plan on waiting much longer than that."

"What if your bride-to-be wants a big wedding?"

"She can have a big wedding with somebody else. I think a wedding is between two people—a man and a woman. After we're married, after we've had our private honeymoon together, I guess I'd want to give a big party for our family and friends. But no big society affair," he added, giving her a hard stare.

"Winfield and I went to a wedding consultant, and she said to plan a decent no-frills wedding would take at least a year," Jewell said dismally. "And longer if we wanted something nice. When my father died, the consultant had just sent me swatches of fabric to choose the color for the bridesmaids' dresses. I'd nearly forgotten that engagement had anything to do with marriage.''

''Wedding consultant? You have to have a wedding consultant to plan how to promise you'll stay together?''

''She was from Jacksonville. Did all the good weddings. Winfield and I finally agreed to use her six months ago. She thought we could get a date set up for sometime this next June.''

''Nine months from now?'' Clay chuckled. ''A lot can happen to a couple in that amount of time,'' he observed.

''In our case, we broke up,'' Jewell said. ''And I don't think money was the whole reason.''

''Really? You think it was coincidental that he broke up with you the day your father's will is read?''

''No, it's just, well, we were never in love. I don't know how to admit this, but I was an old maid. He was a confirmed bachelor. We didn't get together consciously because of that, but I think it must have been in the backs of our heads. And I think both our families were relieved when we got engaged. Rumors were going 'round that I was... I was...''

''What?''

''That I wasn't able to settle down to any one thing. That I was flighty and unreliable and couldn't stick with anything.''

''How'd that rumor develop?''

''Oh, quite reasonably, I suppose. I had my coming out, and a girl's supposed to find her husband within a year or so. I just never fell in love—I don't know why. All the best men of Mississippi were courting me, but I didn't have much interest in any one of them. They bored me after a while. And that's the same with school. I never can stick with anything. I'm not stupid. I'm just..."

"You're not challenged," Clay provided.

"That's a nice way of putting it."

"Well, maybe that's what your father saw," Clay said. "In the will, he makes it pretty clear that he expected your life to follow one of two directions— marriage to Winfield or being on your own. Maybe your father knew, as well as you did, that you weren't in love with Winfield. And he wanted you to make a choice. If you weren't going to marry Winfield, he wanted you to have to find something to do with your life. Having money can make you free, but it can also make you lazy as all get-out. When you don't have to finish school because your survival depends on it, you'll never graduate. If you don't have to work because your survival depends on it, you'll always hit the snooze alarm and never have the hungry ambition to succeed."

She lay down on the grass so that her head was close to his; she felt his body warmth like a source of energy separate and distinct from the sun. The grass beneath her smelled sweet and new.

"But, Clay, I'm scared."

"We're all scared, darlin'. It's just some of us don't show it as much as others."

His fingers pulled hers into his grasp. She felt comforted by the contact, even more so than she would have from anyone else's suffocating hug. She closed her eyes, blinded by the bright orange of sunlight behind her eyelids.

"When my father left us," Clay said, "I wasn't sure what to do. I was young. My mother worked every night at a truck stop. I was responsible for the kids from the minute we got home from school—making sure they got their homework done, giving them dinner, getting them ready for bed. I was scared then, but not half as scared as when I realized my own mother wasn't up to taking care of us. She needed more help. I needed to work. I needed to be a man. Boy becomes a man too early, I think he loses the hang of having fun. Important skill, knowing how to have fun. As for a woman—" he looked at her across the grass "—a woman who becomes a woman too late..."

Jewell opened her eyes. "If you're asking..."

"I wasn't asking."

"The heck you weren't."

"I was just telling you that it's a whole lot different when a woman gambles everything—on a man or even on a job. You've never gambled like that. With all your education, you've always held back from gambling with your life. And as for men, have you ever had to say that you were throwing away everything for his love?"

"No," she admitted. "But have you? With a woman?"

"No. But I've had responsibilities. I've gambled everything for those responsibilities."

"Your sisters and brothers?"

He nodded.

"And now that's over. They're all graduated and have jobs. What do you want to do with the rest of your life?"

He sat up and Jewell tugged at his arm. He turned to her, his face suddenly intense. Then he leaned over her, his strong, hard body pressing against her own. There was no mistaking his intentions. And she had enough warning to be indignant, to cry out her virtue or at least her unwillingness, but she couldn't.

Instead, she felt her lips go dry as bone, and she licked them with her tongue and felt her mouth's anticipation.

"The rest of my life?" he asked. "I want to have my own business, all mine, made from my hard work. I want a house full of children who call me Daddy and trust that I'll be there for them as surely as they trust the sun to rise and set. And I want to make love—and maybe this is the impossible part—to a woman who works at my side during the day, showers our kids with love and who can't keep her hands off of me once the lights are out."

She moaned softly, not because of the words but because of the tone—the intensity, the power, the demand. She wanted it, wanted him, wanted to be taken, to give in to something, someone, more powerful than herself. She forgot every promise she had made to herself.

About security. About returning to her home. About her reentry to privileged society.

All of that was gone, dust that crumbled in her hand and was scattered by the wind.

And so she invited him, parting her lips and casting her eyes downward, waiting for his touch.

But when it came, its intensity shocked her, having had only the kisses of milk-mild men to prepare her.

Her back arched and bucked and slacked only when his hand pressed against the half moon of her stomach.

His mouth caught hers as she turned away to moan a final, halfhearted protest. But once caught, she was brought down fully to take his lips. They were smooth and yet commanding, brooking no coy, schoolgirlish rebuff. His tongue thrust into her mouth, shocking her with his power and force.

This was no good-night kiss at the door of her home, this was no kiss beneath the mistletoe at a country-club Christmas party, this was no air kiss for the photographer from the society page.

This was the kiss that cavemen gave their women, that the ardent gave their bliss, that the victors gave to their spoils. This was the kiss that told her that he could make her his, make her want him, make her beg for him, if he so cared. Because it was the kind of kiss a woman waits all her life for—the kiss that begs love's surrender, the kiss that pleads and wins love's cause.

Her mouth opened wider, her legs parted with an obedience not to her will but to his hands and her neck arched, offering herself to a welcome predator.

How easy to surrender to him, to give him responsibility for her trembling legs and the swollen juncture that begged to be satisfied. How easy to throw away reason and propriety and good sense—which had obviously not given her much of anything in this world. To exchange it for something baser, something that was not her doing, something she would regard later—so much later—as purely his making. She reveled in his smell, now so musky and not nearly so Ivory-soap clean. A secret victory swelled in her as his desire pressed against her legs. And she felt the tremor of his lips as she knew he himself struggled with whether to take her right here, right now, right away.

He jerked away suddenly, looking into her eyes with ones that glittered with amber fire.

"I can't do this," he said huskily.

"Why not?" she said, hurt in pride even as she knew that she shouldn't have flirted so close to the edge of propriety. Although what good propriety did her now, she couldn't say.

"Because you'd be using me."

She bolted upright and crossed her arms over her chest, covering her traitorous nipples.

"What?" she demanded, outraged. "I think it's the other way around."

Clay shook his head. "You're looking for something in your life," he explained with ragged control. "You're looking for something to save you, to make you forget for a little while, somebody to help you back on your feet. And God knows I've got a soft spot for hard-luck stories. But tell me something, if you got your father's money back tomorrow, would you ever want to see me again?"

"Haven't you ever had brief affairs, one-night stands?"

"Yes, but that's not what you're about. You're about forever. And if we start playing for keeps now, you'll always think of me as something you went to because there wasn't anyplace else to go."

Jewell opened her mouth to say that of course she was no snob, that she would always care for him, that money didn't mean that much to her, that it had always been her father's love and not his money that she chased.

That she had thought she'd been robbed, and now it looked as if she had only been disinherited. Sad story but perfectly legal.

She suddenly flashed onto a half-dozen images. Places and situations where he wouldn't belong. The country club. The New Year's Eve party at Pont-chartreaux. The Magnolia Ball. The cotillion parties. The intimate dinners and brunches and garden teas.

"You will always think of me as a consolation prize to the rest of your life," Clay said. "You've had a big shock this afternoon."

"No, that's not true," Jewell protested. "You're not a consolation prize. You're not second-best to any man."

"I know that. But you need a little time to realize that. And I won't have you until you do."

She closed her eyes, willing the aching longing of her sex to subside.

"Let's go get some dinner," Clay said briskly, wiping his hands of errant slips of grass. He stood up and held out his hand to aid her.

She took his hand and mourned the unanswered swell of her sexual center. She had never felt this way, but she sensed it would be many hours before her body was brought back into line.

"Where are we going?" she asked with more nonchalance than she felt.

"A diner on the way to work," he said. "Remember, we still have to cash out the stations. But you'll get to meet Martha, one of my favorite friends. She makes the best catfish. She loves to cook for me. Thinks of me as a grandson she never had. And she's even expecting you."

Jewell felt a sudden visceral streak of meanness—he had brought her to the brink and then had abandoned her.

"Freeloading again?" she asked innocently.

He opened his mouth as if he had angry words to say, but just as suddenly, he shut up. And then, as his eyes returned to their sparkling bronze hue, he laughed.

"Princess, I could take you out for dinner every night for a month and never pay a dime."

Somehow, his words comforted even as they revolted her.

It was much easier to blind herself to him than to see him clearly. Much easier to dismiss him than to have to give him serious thought. Much easier to still hang on to the idea that somehow, some way, someday, she would return to the upper reaches of Mississippi society than to realize that she was no better than the homeless her brother cared for.

MAYBE HE WAS RIGHT.

Maybe Clay could get a free meal every night for a month.

They went out to diners or roadhouses similar to his brother's. Martha, the first of their hosts, was a white-haired, moon-faced woman who shrieked with delight when Clay walked into her tiny redbrick diner. She fussed over Clay and complained that Jewell was too skinny. She set down platters overflowing with catfish and hush puppies, all the while decrying imagined faults and weaknesses of her far-flung grandchildren who, as Jewell listened, appeared to have nothing wrong with them.

And when it came time to leave, there was no check asked for and none given.

And that was how it worked out everywhere Clay went, every day they spent together. He had friends in every hamlet, every corner of the road. Every man knew him—Clay asked after every wife, child, pet dog and incoming crop. Every woman knew him—and the narrow-eyed looks Jewell received made her realize that she resisted what other women would gladly fight for.

And the tension between them increased every day as she grew more certain that the price of slipping between his sheets and letting his hot, callused hands rake across her body was to give up her dream—the dream of returning to Pontchartreaux, of returning to her father's home and protection of his money, of returning to the world, the social circle in which she had been raised.

It was a far-off dream, but somehow, the more she read through her father's will—searching each time for some mistake or clue to wrongdoing—the more determined she became to prove wrong the bare terms of her disinheritance. But sometimes, she caught herself spilling tears on the pages as she struggled to come to terms with her father's death. It had been expected, she had thought herself prepared. And yet...

Clay watched but said nothing. Nothing when he found her at the cash register, reading the legal document, checking off important parts with a yellow highlighter pen. Nothing when she took out his copy of *Black's Law Dictionary* to look up terms she didn't understand. Nothing when she stared out onto the wavering heat rising up from the road with an expression as faraway as the North Pole.

She went to bed each night, and he rode his motorcycle until the earliest morning hours. Then, shoving the dogs between them, he claimed exactly half—no more and no less—of his bed. But never her body. They never talked about it and they studiously avoided any body contact.

Somehow, he seemed to know exactly what she thought of him, as rankling as the truth was.

Sexy as all get-out, but not worth the price.

She would return to Pontchartreaux.

He would not be with her when she did.

## Chapter Seven

"There's nothing wrong with this will," said Thomas Fogerty, peering at her from over his bifocals. He turned from the last page back to the first and neatly placed the stapled, well-thumbed will on the far edge of his desk, near where Jewell sat. He pulled out the middle drawer of his desk. "You know, Jewell, you look a little peaked. You've been obsessing about this a little too long. I have a few thousand dollars of discretionary money I could loan you—interest pegged at the prime rate, of course."

"What?" Jewell asked absently, sliding her copy of the will into her tote bag. Black linen—well, not real linen, actually rayon acetate—from Payless—on sale for $24.99—the big splurge of her first paycheck.

Her next stop after speaking with Thomas was going to be L'Hermitage, where she'd pay off that I.O.U. And then she'd be back where she started two weeks before.

Broke.

"Thomas, I've read through this will a hundred times and I'm a little suspicious. I mean, he doesn't leave much to Mia."

"She already has the carriage house. And she has already put aside money in a pension fund. I did the paperwork for it—she's set for life. Don't worry about her."

"Well, also in the will, I noticed that he didn't leave anything to Rev. Copland's church. He's gone there every Sunday since he was a child. I can't believe he wouldn't leave the church something."

"Charles has made many gifts over the years. He funded the renovation of the chapel and the refurbishing of the Civil War Veterans' cemetery. He's done a lot. And I haven't seen Rev. Copland in here complaining."

"So there's nothing, absolutely nothing, wrong with this will?"

"Nothing at all."

"And you don't find anything suspicious about this will?"

Thomas took a deep breath. "No. Not at all," he said, clearly irritated.

"So what am I supposed to do with my life?" Jewell challenged.

"Maybe since you're nearly family to me, we should think of this as a graduation gift," Thomas said, placing his checkbook in front of him and slipping the cap off his fountain pen with a flourish. "Graduation from the school of hard knocks. Don't even worry about paying it back. Just get on with your life. Get your hair done, buy some decent clothes and go back to Memphis. Finish up school, get a real job, find yourself a nice husband. That's what you're supposed to do with your life."

She took the check from him and studied it.

"Why now? Why are you giving me money now? Two weeks ago, you couldn't give me the guest room."

"Because I thought you had sense enough to get out of town and make a new life for yourself—staying in my house would only prolong the pain of having to be independent. But now I can't stand to see what you're doing with your life!"

"And what exactly am I doing with my life?" she demanded coolly.

"You've shacked up with a man who is no gentleman," Thomas said, dropping his usual dainty way with words. "You're working at a gas station, which has got to be the most lower-class thing I can ever imagine short of working the streets, and you look like hell, too. Especially your hair."

He barked all this out with all the indignity of a father berating a teen.

"What's wrong with my hair?"

"Take a look," Thomas said, lifting his head in the direction of the round, gilded Federalist-style mirror on the wall.

With as much regality as she could muster, Jewell roused herself from the armchair and took a look at the damage.

Roots.

Brown ones. Easily an inch or more long.

She hadn't had the money or even the inclination to worry about going to a colorist. Her personal colorist, the one she had seen every four weeks without fail when she had had the money, would cost more than two weeks' pay. She looked down at her nails. Buffed, clean—but short. She looked carefully at her face. Unblemished and unadorned, with just a hint of clear lip gloss. The dozen "essential" cosmetics—mascara, tinted moisturizer, eyeliner, lipstick and pencil, blushes and powders—long since forgotten at the bottom of her purse.

The expensive Prada bag—the one now used by Samson as a pillow for his head.

In the past few weeks, there had been some changes in her, and she hadn't even noticed. The least of it her hair.

"I do need to get my hair done," she conceded.

"You need to move out of that squalor and get a nice job."

"Tell me what a nice job is."

"Work at one of the dress shops or at the historical society or at the library. Or go back to school. Finish some degree, any degree. Just do something more in keeping with your social position."

"My social position as what?"

"The daughter of Charles Whittington," Thomas answered exasperatedly.

"Well, none of those places would have me."

He waved away her objections. "I'm sure they would if you asked again. And definitely move out of that man's bed right now. You know, there's plenty of girls your age who've had their little romp with some local boy. But those girls have sense enough to keep it discreet and know when to cut it off. You're doing everything out in the open. People are talking about you, and your reputation is going to be harmed forever. No man in his right mind, no decent man, will want to marry you if…"

"I'm not sleeping with him, if that's what you're asking."

Thomas looked at her as if she had just told him that a cottonmouth was crawling up his leg.

"It doesn't even matter if you are or you aren't. I won't argue with you about a fact that looks as plain as day to me. You look like you're sleeping with him. And he has a reputation."

"He does?"

"A hard man. Hardworking, I'll give him credit for that. But his father was a no-'count, and I believe breeding shows. Clay's had a string of women, Jewell, you're not the first."

She turned away, not wanting Thomas to see her blush.

"If you worked at a more suitable place," Thomas continued, "a decent man would feel free to court you, and you could be accepted back by your friends, although, of course, in a different way."

She whirled around to stare at him, eyes sparkling with fury.

"You mean, pick something safe and genteel to do and wait for a man to pick me up as a charity case and then, and only then, will my so-called friends—the ones who haven't returned my phone calls since the funeral—like me again?"

"Not that harshly, but that's pretty much the idea."

"This is not the nineteenth century, Thomas!" she shrieked, not even caring as his secretary, Mary, opened the door a crack and then closed it. "Nobody helped me, nobody offered me a hand and Clay did. He helped me out when I was worse off than a stray dog on the street. He gave me a job, he gave me a place to live when all of my friends were telling their house-keepers to make up excuses when I called. He's been a gentleman, even if you don't think so. And he works hard, he's nice to people whether they can do something for him or not and I admire him more than I ever admired Winfield, more than I ever did you and almost as much as I ever did my own—''

The word *father* was almost out of her lips before she stopped herself.

"Jewell, I think you're in love with this man," Thomas said coldly. "And that's a very dangerous notion."

She opened her mouth. *Of course not. Don't be ridiculous. I'm not that kind of a woman.* But the words stuck in her throat.

It seemed a betrayal too deep to say anything, anything at all. The office fell silent—except for the sterling tick-tock of the grandfather clock and the scratch of Thomas's fountain pen on his check. When he was done, he carefully put the cap on his pen and ripped the check off its pad with a flourish.

"Here's five thousand to get you started," he said. "And if you need more, you come on back to me, but I think you'll find this enough to get you started. No, no, don't thank me now. Thank me when we're celebrating your wedding—to someone suitable. I'm counting on you letting me have the first dance."

She licked her lips. Five thousand. Nice job. Nice husband. Nice life someday back in the circle of friends and interlocking families that made up Mississippi upper-crust society.

Wasn't that what she had been reading and rereading this will for? Wasn't that what she was here right now in Fogerty's office for? Wasn't that everything she aspired to and worked for and dreamed of?

She thought of the check that Michael had left for her—twenty thousand dollars. She looked at Thomas, who mopped up beads of sweat from his forehead with a starched handkerchief. If she didn't take this, she knew, there would be no further handouts.

She impulsively grabbed at her tote bag.

"Keep your damn money, Thomas. I work for mine now."

"Jewell!"

She slammed the door behind her and started to march for the lobby.

But Thomas's secretary, Mary, grabbed her by the elbow and motioned her to silently follow her to the ladies' room.

"You're Clay's friend, right?" Mary asked furtively once they were inside.

"Yeah," Jewell replied cautiously.

"Well, I thought you might be interested in this," Mary said, and shoved a newspaper clipping into Jewell's hand.

"What?"

But Mary had already slipped out of the rest room, leaving behind the thin whoosh of the door.

Jewell looked at the clipping. On one side were the Help Wanted ads, on the other an obituary for some attorney from Jackson. Jewell shook her head in wry disbelief.

Her father's lawyer wanted her to get a job, but only the secretary had had sense enough to show her how to do it. Classifieds. Help Wanted. Even though most of the ads asked for secretarial skills, which Jewell most definitely did not possess. She looked for the wastebasket, then realized that if she threw it away, the secretary might see it and would think that she was snubbing her advice. So she crumpled up the newspaper and shoved it into her tote without another thought.

She walked out of the law offices of Thomas Fogerty and Associates a poor woman. But a woman of independence. Her future lay ahead of her, uncertain. And her past was gone, nothing left but memories.

THE EFFECT WAS like that of a surprise party.

"Oh, my God!" Jewell cried out as she stepped into the apartment an hour later. Samson and Delilah crowded at her feet, got their perfunctory pats on the head and walked away.

They couldn't understand the excitement.

"Do you like it?" Clay asked, suddenly boyish. Jewell realized that she had never before seen him show uncertainty. He wanted her approval; he needed her approval.

As if she meant something to him.

As if she were more than a stray he picked up on the road.

Her heart skipped.

She twirled slowly around, taking it all in.

He had done it for her, a tribute laid at her feet, a tribute that two weeks ago would have made her shrug with disdain but now made her blush with delight.

The eggshell walls smarted from the two coats of white paint.

The lace curtains fluttered in the breeze, splattering the walls with delicate shadows.

The bamboo-and-cane furniture was clearly secondhand but well polished. A couch, two armchairs and a coffee table.

A brightly colored rag rug sprawled across the hardwood floor—the slats glimmering with lemon-scented polish.

And, she noted, the bathroom was immaculate—a Battenberg lace shower curtain covering the thin plastic liner, white plush towels hanging from hooks and a wicker laundry basket by the sink.

"How did you manage . . . ?"

He smiled, embarrassed and happy at the same time.

"I had a little money put away. I figured it was time to stop living like a rat—don't worry, I know you're leaving soon," Clay said. "But I thought I'd try to make things a little more comfortable while you stay. Besides, I was getting a little tired of being pushed out of bed by the dogs. You three take up a lot of room, and I've spent too many nights trying to get comfortable on the couch."

She looked at the bed, forlornly stripped of its sheets.

"What're you doing with the bed?"

He looked away. "I've bought twins," he said. "Guy's coming in a few hours with them. I thought we could buy some sheets tonight."

"Twin beds? Just like Lucy and Ricky?"

"They were married," Clay corrected. "We're . . . just friends."

"Still," she said, staring at the bed. Her voice fell to a whisper. "They managed to get Little Ricky somehow."

She walked around the room, feeling his eyes on her. They both avoided the stripped bed.

"I talked to the lawyer today," she said.

"What'd he say?"

"He offered me a check for five thousand. I didn't take it."

"I wouldn't have taken it, either."

"His secretary gave me a section of the classified ads to look for a job."

"I thought you already have one—right here."

"This one isn't . . ." Her voice trailed off.

"Listen, work that's got to be done is always good."

She looked at him, his hair made like a halo by the sun streaming through the window behind him. She noticed, irrelevantly, that he had washed the windows and they sparkled as beautifully as the most expensive Waterford crystal.

He was a hard man. Kind to a fault, friend of the helpless—but inside, he was like steel.

Except maybe for some secret part that had melted before her. A one-room apartment on top of a gas station couldn't be home, shouldn't be home.

It wasn't respectable.

It wasn't suitable.

He wasn't respectable.

He wasn't suitable.

But she knew there wasn't any other place on earth she wanted to be.

And there wasn't any other man on earth she wanted to be with more. It was almost a relief to have no way back home. Back to her father's way of life.

"Clay, call the guy," she said. "Tell him you don't want the twins."

He stared at her long and hard. She met his gaze and then, embarrassed by his intensity, by his fierce longing, looked away.

"I'm not sleeping on the couch anymore," he said huskily. "The dogs have got to go. They can learn to sleep on the floor. You know what this means, you know how people will talk."

"I know," she said breathlessly. "And I think that any gossip that's going 'round is already far ahead of us."

They didn't touch. She changed into a pair of blue jeans and a work shirt that had Bill stitched on the right pocket. She acted as if he weren't there, leaving his gaze unacknowledged. Even when she heard his sharp intake of breath as she briefly revealed the lacy pink demibra and matching panties.

He made the phone call to cancel delivery of the beds while she washed her face in the bathroom. Thomas was right—her hair made her look like a streetwalker, and she realized she had been a blonde so long that she had nearly forgotten that her natural hair color was brown. She tried to remember if she had liked the brown hair, then decided that she, like her friends, began coloring her hair when she was too young to know the difference. Only because every Southern princess should be as blond as Cinderella.

And she was Cinderella in reverse, finding her prince far from the ball and the horse-drawn carriages.

When she finished with a light touch of gloss, she opened the bathroom door to find him putting worn, soft white sheets on the bed. She helped him by putting the pillowcases on.

When the bed was complete, her fingers lingered at the top sheet's hand-stitched hem of lace.

"I can't make love to you now," Clay said, his voice hoarse and aching. "We have work to do and we can't neglect it. I want to take a long time. I want to make it last. And I won't leap up from this bed. I want to fall asleep with you in my arms."

She knew what he meant, and she knew how important it was for him to do what was right before what was pleasurable.

"Let's go," she said.

They did what they always did. Cashed out the registers, counting the money and reconciling it with the register tape. They chatted in turn with the three other station managers about the day, accepting coffee from one, a soda from another and home-baked apple pie from the last. On the long drives between stations, they talked only of business. They stopped at Al's Roadhouse, but when Al put two beers in front of them, Jewell and Clay both declined.

Without speaking, they had agreed to keep their minds clear. They wanted to make love, and the tension between them as they waited for the opportunity built like a delicious staircase of pleasure.

They didn't talk about it, and yet, everyone around them seemed to know—even though Clay and Jewell never touched or boasted or kissed or told. A crackle of excitement surrounded them. And just as Clay was able to bring happiness and security and calmness to others, so too was he able to communicate his sense of love's fruition.

At Al's Roadhouse, couples who had felt their marriage's low points looked at their beloved with new hope. Men who hadn't had the courage to introduce themselves to a woman they admired suddenly found their voice. Women who thought that it was going to be just another night out with the girls found themselves drawn to the dance floor and to the realm of possibility. Old men recalled childhood sweethearts, and women put on lipstick that had been sitting at the bottom of their purses for months.

The band lingered on slow, moody music—the kind that lovers love. But Clay and Jewell didn't stay. They had a quick, light meal and waved to Al without waiting for him to find a slow moment for the nightly gossip.

And when Jewell breathed in the magnolia-drenched air of the parking lot, she knew what she was getting into. And she knew it would be difficult to walk away from—even if she were ever given the opportunity.

They drove in total silence. When Clay parked the truck under the willow out back of the garage, he took her hand in his. The touch, coming after so many hours of anticipation, struck Jewell to the very core of her being.

"Jewell, you understand you walk up those stairs and do what I think we will do, I'm never going to let you go."

"You won't have to," Jewell answered.

"Oh?"

"My fight for my father's money is over," she said. "You're just going to have to take me as I am. A former heiress. An ex-princess. If you want me for my money, you better find another woman."

"I don't want another woman and, frankly, I'm happy you don't have any money. One day, you'll wear diamonds again. One day, you'll have your own home. One day, you'll have the pretty clothes that you like. But I want those diamonds to come from me, the house to come from me and everything to come from honest work."

He opened the truck door and got out. Jewell opened her door to follow him, but he came around to her side and picked her up. After waiting so long for physical contact, she felt as if she had been shot through with a current of electricity so strong it scrambled her senses. She put her arms around his neck, and felt there was no give, no softness—except when he looked at her, his warm eyes melting for her, just for her.

She had never known power like this, power that only came by surrender of self, relinquishment of all claims to wealth, prestige, security. Her dominion over him was purely in her capitulation, which was peace as she had never known it.

HE KICKED the truck's door closed and effortlessly carried her across the lot to the stairs. She held on to him, at first from fear of the awkwardness of being carried—as she had not been since a child in her nanny's arms—and then she held him because she wanted to. Because she wanted to be held by him, to give herself completely to him, to let go.

She realized in her relinquishment just how much energy she had used to rein in desire and feeling and longing and wanting. And she was startled as she understood that she was about to give herself to him, to open to him, more fully and completely than she had to any man before.

For there had been other men. Winfield, with his dry caresses, and one other man who had been eminently suitable and terribly boring. Clay was not boring—even his handshake was enough to excite a woman.

He paused at the top of the staircase to kiss her with seeming chastity on her forehead, warning her that he would do nothing less than take her and brand her as his own.

Forever and ever.

There would be no more suitable young men. No more perfectly proper courtships. No more daydreaming about what china to choose for registering at Gump's.

She had already tumbled into a different world, but her father's lawyer had given her a lifeline, a way out, a chance to climb from where she had fallen. She hadn't taken it, and now, if she lay down with Clay, she knew she never would leave.

Did he really have that kind of hold over her that she would have given up her last and only chance to regain her former life?

Yes. Yes. Yes! she thought exultantly.

He flung aside the homey quilt and let her slide from his arms to the worn, soft sheets—so much finer than silk. He stood above her, between her legs, hesitant as his eyes appraised her.

"I don't know how to make love to a lady," he said softly, gently in a way that belied the hard sex that swelled beneath his jeans.

"Oh, yes, you do," Jewell murmured, reaching her hand out to pull him down on top of her. "You do, Clay."

He pulled her head back, his fingers lightly touching her hair in command, for he knew that she would obey his every loving stroke. He kissed her sunblushed neck and then, tugging at the shoulders of her blouse, inflamed each inch of exposed flesh with his demanding lips. Eyes closed against the unbearable pleasure, Jewell felt the buttons of her shirt give way, heard one pop from its stay and bounce on the floor.

The glory of it! The wanton power and pleasure of offering herself to Clay and of taking from him nothing but pleasure. For there was nothing he could give her, except himself, except the moment of ecstasy, except this simple bed.

With apparent reluctance, he lifted himself up from her, and her heart galloped as she thought he would take from her this chance at pleasures unknown. But he kept her pinned down with a hard thigh pressed against her sex and he yanked his shirt over his head.

She stared, drinking in his muscular chest, browned by the sun. She worshipped him as women have always worshipped the godlike perfection of a man's body.

And it was a worship well returned. His eyes turned lighter, to amber, and seemed to liquefy as he caressed and possessed and honored her naked flesh without laying a finger on her.

And then he unbuttoned his jeans.

"Clay, let me," she said.

He paused, searched her eyes and seemed to question that she would want anything further from lovemaking than to be a passive recipient of his adoration.

But Jewell leaned forward, releasing his trapped sex by unzipping the jeans and pushing both jeans and briefs down to his thighs. He stepped back for only a moment to complete the task.

And then he stood before her. Proud, hard and strong—even if there was some part of him that wondered at her willingness to share his bed. His eyes met hers and held.

"Is this just a little romp for you?" he asked huskily. "Because if it is, I warn you, Jewell, if I touch you now, you'll be mine. Forever."

"Then touch me," Jewell answered recklessly. "Make me yours. I want that."

"You know everything you're giving up to be with me? You'll be my woman—not just behind closed doors, not just until you have some cash in your pocket, not just for the moment."

"I've given all that up already."

He stepped forward and placed his palm upon the juncture of her legs. Jewell's mouth tensed as she tried to control her bucking, impatient longing.

She didn't know how, but in moments, she was naked before him. Her lacy ecru bra and panties on the floor, her jeans in a crumpled heap beside them. She was ready for him, hot and slick and open, and her mind reeled with images of that moment when he would enter her.

But he didn't. He whom she surrendered to now knelt before her and used his mouth to lure her deeper into the foreign territory of the pleasures of the flesh.

When she thought she would tumble from the precipice, he pulled back from her.

"Oh, no," she whimpered, beyond thinking, beyond reason, beyond anything except the sensations he evoked.

"No?" he queried.

Jewell panicked, realizing how very much she didn't want to stop, how very much she wanted, needed to continue.

"Yes," she said after calming herself.

He waited no longer, but thrust into her deeply. And she felt it as deeply as if she were a virgin, and it was, in fact, as if she were because she could never have known or imagined such a feeling as when he thrust and stroked teasingly out from her and then repeated the commandment to pleasure all over again.

Again. Again. And more.

Her legs curled around his back to encourage him.

At first, her eyes squeezed shut because she couldn't bear to meet his possessive gaze, and then she opened her eyes to him, knowing that she could only be fully taken by him if she gave everything, every part of herself to him. Including that final treasure, that final relinquishment—her eyes, so that every part of her soul was his.

His eyes met hers, at first hard like an eagle's and then softening at each moment of impact.

Her flesh softened, then began to pulsate, repeating his every stroke with a contraction of her own. She heard herself cry out, as if from a faraway place, and then—squeezing him to her innermost part as she felt the thunderous ecstasy—there was nothing left of herself. Nothing that was not apart from him, nothing that was not tingling with his touch. At that very moment, he cried out and, with a final, anguished thrust, pulsated within her.

He collapsed against her, still careful to hold his weight up on his elbows. His heart was beating powerful and triumphant against her skin. His head burrowed against the side of her neck, and he breathed warm sighs upon her skin.

At last, his heart stilled to a quiet, steady pace, and he looked up at her, searching for the doubts and regret that weren't there. Then he picked her up in his arms and tenderly laid her at the center of the bed, fluffing up a soft pillow for her head and pulling the quilt around her shoulders.

He curled himself around her from behind, one arm flung possessively around her waist, another slipping beneath the pillow that cradled her head. His hard, muscular body framed hers, releasing the scent of musk and satisfaction, a thin drizzling of sweat evaporating in the still Mississippi heat.

Outside, cicadas and bullfrogs chorused—with an occasional interruption by a speeding car. All like a rhythmic lullaby.

She felt as passive and protected as a baby, exhausted from their lovemaking. She slipped into sleep and then back out, always conscious of his arms locked around her.

Minutes later, he hardened against her back.

"Mmm. Again?" she murmured.

"Darlin', that was just for openers," he said, and pulled her head back so that he could rain kisses upon her naked flesh.

## Chapter Eight

The hands on the alarm clock might have stopped circling and the earth might have stood still in its orbit unnoticed and others, more sensible folk, might have slept and dreamed secure.

But Jewell and Clay made love, creating a new world of heat and light and passion that transformed—again and again—until they could not count the times they turned to each other. The question "more?" asked with a caress and answered with a moan of delight.

The lines between one moment of pleasure and the next blurred. He brought her to orgasm so many ways, with his hands, his mouth, his sex and yet, often he did so as his own body rested from the demands of ecstasy. Then she would touch him, and he would be ready—though moments before he was convinced that he couldn't. Not even one more time.

But there was always more.

Until, at last, it was dawn and their bodies finally demanded sleep.

"How will I ever get the energy to work?" Jewell groaned.

"You'll find it," Clay said confidently.

Jewell had opened herself to him as only the truest virgin could—she had never known possession by a man, and it was clear, from how her body responded to him, that she wanted to be possessed by him. Only him.

That shocked him as he thought back to the dirty, sun-punished youth who had worked on the grounds of her father's house and how he had only glimpsed her from a distance. She had been his ideal, his dream of what womanhood was, a fantasy.

She still was.

But now the fantasy had flesh. He slept with strange alertness, awakening fully every few minutes to remind himself: she was here, she was with him, she was in his arms, she was his, she wanted him, she wanted him, she wanted him alone.

How long she would be his, he couldn't say.

He had so confidently told her the previous night that she would be his forever.

But he knew she might return to where she had come from—the different world of privilege and money. Given the chance, she would abandon him and he wouldn't follow.

And he knew, in his heart, that he would always be hers.

Funny how the captor becomes the captive.

He would miss her spunk, her resourcefulness, miss watching how she had grown from a spoiled brat into a woman. But he might have to watch all this, again, from a distance.

A distance of sweat and work and money and class.

"Will we be together now?" she asked. "I mean, was this just a one-night stand?"

He chuckled, deep in his chest. "No, this lasts as long as you want it to," he said.

"As long as I want to? What about what you want? Why do you say that? Do you think I'm leaving?"

"You will when something better comes along," he said, not feeling bitterness so much as resignation.

"Clay, I have something to show you," she said suddenly.

He groaned as she pulled out of his arms. He leaned up on one elbow and admired her body as she picked up her tote bag from the table. He felt a stirring for her in his loins, and was surprised—how much passion could he feel for one woman?

She sat down on the edge of the bed, seemingly unconcerned about her nakedness but with the unconscious pride in her body that only a woman truly loved feels. Clay smiled and cupped her round breasts in his hands. She swatted his hand away with playful indignation.

"Clay, stop, I want you to see something," she said, pulling from the tote a stack of papers that he recognized as her father's will. A scrap of newspaper fluttered out and landed on the quilt next to him.

"Not this again," he groaned. "Don't tell me you've got some new plan to get your money."

"No, I want you to see me rip this in half," she said. "I told you last night that there aren't any more chances to get my father's money back, and I'm not going to try to snare a husband just for his money. I'm telling you, Clay, it's over. This will is history."

She held up the will, in two hands, ready to rip in two when Clay picked up the newspaper clipping.

"What's this?"

"Just a classified ad that Thomas's secretary gave me," Jewell said dismissively. "She seemed rather furtive about it. I don't know why. It's just a list of jobs. They're all for people who have office skills, which I don't. But it was nice of her all the same."

Clay looked at it more closely, then turned it over.

"She wasn't handing you jobs, Jewell," he said. "She was handing you an obituary."

Jewell put down the will and grabbed the scrap of newspaper from his hand. She studied it.

"So what? It's the obituary of a lawyer in Jackson who died six months ago and is survived by a wife, a son named Beauregard and a daughter named Louella."

"That's not the important point," Clay said. He pointed at the date at the top of the page. "George Witherspoon. Died six months ago. Law offices in Jackson."

"Respected member of the community. Survived by three sons and nine grandchildren," Jewell read impatiently. "So what?"

"You know George Witherspoon."

"I do?"

"Look at your father's will," Clay said curtly. "Last page."

Jewell flipped back the pages of the will.

"George Witherspoon executed the will," she said. "That makes sense. Daddy was getting treatments in Jackson, so he just used a lawyer from there. I still don't get it."

"Look closer."

Clay got up from the bed, and Jewell briefly admired his hard, proud body. He pulled on his briefs and jeans and went to stand by the window. He was perfection, a god, a man who had made his body a temple—but now Jewell wasn't paying attention.

"Oh, my God, Clay! I figured it out. He was dead two months before the will was signed," she said excitedly. "This lawyer couldn't have witnessed my daddy signing the will."

"Seems so," Clay said, his voice strangely distant and sad.

"That means the will is a fraud!" Jewell said excitedly. "I knew it all along! I just didn't know how it was wrong, but I knew it was wrong. Now I have proof."

"You sure do."

"Oh, wow! This is wonderful!" Jewell cried out, and she leapt into the air. "My father didn't leave me penniless. He meant to leave me everything. Clay, we're rich!"

And just as suddenly, she stilled. "You think this means I'm leaving, don't you?"

"I wouldn't expect you to stay."

Jewell's mouth went dry. "But why can't you come with me?"

Clay looked out the window. "I'm not used to the finer things in life, Jewell."

She pulled the quilt around her because suddenly, even after a night in which she had had no shame, she needed to be clothed.

"Clay, I want you," she said pleadingly, hating herself for begging, but knowing that she had no choice. She couldn't imagine life without him—wasn't it strange that she had only known him a few short weeks?—and she would do anything, say anything, to keep him.

She loved him, she knew now. And yet, there was some part of her, some foolish pride that wouldn't say the word until she had had reassurance from him.

Reassurance that didn't look as if it was forthcoming. He simply stared at her, his eyes narrowed and dark.

She turned away and began putting on her clothes.

"I'll call Thomas," she said brightly. "As soon as I explain..."

"You'd be a fool to do it," Clay said curtly. He leaned against the windowsill and stared at her with hard, unreadable eyes. "Thomas Fogerty already knows about this. The legal community is small—he would have known when Witherspoon died."

"So he knew the will was a fraud but he won't do anything about it?" Jewell asked disbelievingly. "He's a family friend, he would never...unless..."

"He knows. It would have been a lot easier for whoever put this will together to have Thomas's signature at the bottom of the will. This forgery of Witherspoon's signature after his death was a next-best thing. So that means Thomas Fogerty came in on the scheme after the fact—there's got to be some reason he was lured into it."

"It doesn't matter about Thomas, I suppose. The important thing is to walk into court and ask that this will be declared a fraud."

"And then what? You might inherit with your brother equally under state law if there's no other will saying otherwise."

"But my brother's the one who probably set up the fraud in the first place."

"Tough to prove that it's him with nothing but this signature. I think you better find the real will and find out if your father left anything that makes perfectly clear he didn't want to write a new will."

"How am I going to do that?" Jewell wailed.

"I don't know." Clay shrugged. "Give it a few days. Think carefully before you take any actions. Don't rush things, Jewell, because that's how people make mistakes."

He picked up his shirt and, without another word, he went downstairs to open up. A car horn honked, and hearty greetings were exchanged between Clay and his first customer of the morning. The smell of fresh-brewed coffee wafted up to the apartment.

Jewell sat for several minutes on the bed. She realized that his admonition about not rushing things applied to both of them. He didn't want her to rush into challenging the will without making sure that she would benefit.

And he thought that their lovemaking was a mistake, rushing them both into something he didn't want. He still thought they didn't belong together if she was wealthy—a notion with which she would have agreed just a few days ago.

She had felt so close to him, so much a part of him, and it had all been destroyed by a piece of paper. An obituary of an attorney in Jackson. The piece of paper had given her the ammunition to gain her birth-right—while taking away the man she'd grown to love.

"I CAN'T FEED YOU tonight, bro," Al said regretfully, his eyes flickering once over Jewell and then darting back to his brother. "Ma says she needs you. And she's making fried-chicken po'boy sandwiches for dinner."

"Something wrong?" Clay asked.

Al nodded. "I could ask the same of you," he said quietly, tilting his chin toward Jewell.

"Don't," Clay warned.

So close were Clay and Al that, without words, Al knew his brother had laid out his soul to this woman and had been rebuffed. In some way. He could not know the details, and didn't need to. He briefly put his hand on Clay's shoulder.

"Ma says she's got a letter from the bank for you to look at," Al said. "Sounds real bad. Better get over there right quick."

"I'm on my way," Clay said, pulling himself from the bar.

He felt tired and clumsy and muddled in his thinking.

On the other hand, the role of provider, protector, decision maker for the DeVries family came naturally to him. Whether it was a leaky faucet, car trouble or a financial crisis, his mother and siblings called Clay.

He slipped into his worn role as family protector as he walked out to the parking lot and got in the driver's seat of the truck. He felt Jewell get in next to him. He didn't trust himself to look at her.

Seemingly, they were lovers—because neither had said anything that cut the binding ties between them.

Yet, they were not lovers—because the simple touches and caresses of the morning after were absent.

He didn't let his hand graze against hers as they both used the cash register.

He didn't nuzzle her neck as she brought out sandwiches she had fixed upstairs for lunch.

He didn't steal a kiss as the afternoon stretched slow and hot and humid.

He didn't say the words that lovers say, and he broke the silence between them only to tell her that this customer needed to be charged for a brake job, that customer a radiator and it surely was hot, wasn't it?

THE HOUSE WAS a tidy Victorian farmhouse with white siding, blush red shutters and a plush green lawn dotted with lilies of the valley. The windows sparkled dazzlingly with the pink twilight, and on the front lawn stood a wrought-iron chair, love seat and table with implicit invitation for a summer afternoon tea.

Surrounded by a neighborhood of ramshackle ranch houses with brown crab grass and dull and crumbling brick bungalows, the home was like an island of domesticity and grace. The DeVries house was maintained, no doubt, with hard work—lawn care and gardening alone must be several hours a week at least.

And Jewell had no doubt in her mind who did the work. She wondered where Clay found the time.

"Did you live here all your life?" she asked.

"Yeah, all the children were raised here. I'd rather have her in a nicer neighborhood, but Ma says she knows everybody here and loves it."

As the truck pulled up to the side of the white picket fence, the front screen door swung open and a petite older woman in jeans and a paisley silk shirt raced out.

"Clay, Clay, I'm so glad you're here!"

Clay got out of the car and enjoyed her hug, giving her affection and love without reserve. Jewell felt a pang of jealousy course through her.

She had never had that sort of freedom with her father. At moments of great emotion he would merely pat her shoulder and tell her, "Good job."

"Oh, Clay, thank God!" his mom cried out. "You have to take a look at this letter from the bank. It's just awful. It's a disaster. I don't know what to do!"

Although it was clear that she would have smothered him with kisses and hugs forever if he gave her a chance, Clay pulled her arms from around his shoulders and directed her toward the house. Still, he kept one arm firmly around her shoulder, satisfying his mother's desire for contact.

"I'm sure it's just fine," he said soothingly.

Jewell hesitantly got out of the truck.

"Ma, I want you to meet Jewell," Clay said, holding out his free arm to her.

Jewell smiled and held out her hand to shake that of Clay's mother.

"Mrs. DeVries," she said.

"Oh, just call me Ma. Everyone does."

Jewell pulled back her hand and let Ma pull her into a hug.

"I've heard all about you from Al," Ma said as she held Jewell out for inspection. "Darlin', you need a little haircut or at least a touch-up on your roots."

Jewell felt a hot blush explode on her face.

"I, uh, I probably do," she said.

"Well, turn yourself over to me, because I used to be a hairdresser. Clay can read the letter and figure out what to do."

"I thought you were a waitress."

Ma laughed. "Darlin', in this family, you'll find that every one of us has worked every job imaginable in order to make ends meet. Only thing none of us hasn't tried is being president, and I'm sure Clay here would do better than half the men who've held office in the last fifty years."

The trio laughed and, the ice broken, they walked toward the house old friends. Ma showed Jewell the evening primroses tucked under the magnolia tree; the blooms were just opening, as they did every evening as the sun went down. Jewell admired the porch's intricate woodwork, which Ma explained had been handwrought by Clay the summer between his junior and senior years of high school. Clay ushered them into the house, and Jewell wasn't surprised to see that the same meticulous attention to detail and cozy comfort appeared inside, as well as outside. She settled into a wicker armchair and accepted a tall glass of mint-garnished ice tea from Ma while Clay ran upstairs to get the letter from the bank.

It was a house unlike any she had ever seen before, and yet, it was the blueprint for Clay's hasty decorating project at the apartment. Jewell stretched in her chair, and felt more at home than she had in any of the twenty-six rooms of the Whittington mansion.

"Now, what do you want me to do tonight?" Ma asked. "Cut it back to your natural color or bleach the roots to match what your hairdresser's been doing all along?"

Jewell laughed self-consciously. "How do you know I want you to do anything at all?" she asked.

"Because you keep pushing your hair back with your hands like it's all in your way. You're about up to here with it," she added, touching her forehead. "And I think I can help. I always help my boy's friends."

"Is that what we are? Friends?"

"Darlin', I know a little more than you might give me credit for. My Clay's got some feelings for you and he's old enough and has given enough to this family that he should have a chance to go for it. He's good enough for you," Ma added thoughtfully. "You won't find a better man, and I'm being real objective here."

"You are?" Jewell teased lightly.

"Clay's worked to support this family since he was twelve, when my husband walked out on us," Ma said seriously. "He's put three kids through college and graduate school. I've got a son who's a doctor, another who's a lawyer and a daughter who's a professor of anthropology out East. Al's the one who wanted a restaurant, and Clay saved up and bought it for him."

"Is that why Al never charges him for dinner?"

Ma laughed heartily. "Al is so happy doing what he's doing and he's so grateful to Clay that he'll feed

Clay every night for the rest of his life, and he'll feel he still hasn't paid him back. And he's right.''

Jewell felt guilty about every time she had thought of Clay as a freeloader.

"As for the house," Ma continued, "Clay bought me this and always gives me money to add to what I make at the truck stop. He says that if I couldn't work another day of my life, it wouldn't matter. But I hope that some of my other children will be on their feet enough that they can take over helping out Ma. It's Clay's turn now. His turn to get what he wants.''

"And what does he want?''

"You. And his own business.''

"Me?" Jewell said, her throat catching. "How do you know that?''

"Oh, he hasn't said anything, but a momma knows when there's something her boy wants. When my husband first ran out on us, I had a lot of practice at knowing my children wanted things, needed things, that I couldn't give them. Clay's the one who figured out what they wanted and worked to give it to them. They're all self-sufficient, and it's time Clay thought of himself.''

Jewell swallowed. Hard.

She felt as if she were tumbling around in circles, falling from a precipice where she had once thought herself superior to him, and now she realized that she had done little in her life to warrant those feelings. Oh, sure, she had a bachelor's degree and several almost-graduate degrees. Oh, sure, she had been a debutante, presented at the cotillion. Oh, sure, she was schooled in the graces of the upper classes.

But Clay had more-enduring qualities. Hardworking. Determined. Ambitious. Selfless. A provider for his family.

There was a reason he was working at a gas station on the other side of thirty, and it had nothing to do with being unmotivated.

"Why don't you cut it?" Jewell asked suddenly. "Let's get rid of all the bleached part. I'd be kind of curious to see what my natural hair color looks like."

"That's a great idea, much better than coloring it up. Only a woman with nothing but time on her hands can waste it on going in for touch-ups every few weeks."

She took in Jewell's look of appraisal and touched the crown of her brilliant auburn hair proudly.

"That's what my son has gotten me," she said proudly. "A luxury I'd never known before—time. My hair turned white the year my husband left me, and now I work four days a week, and if I want to touch up my roots every week, I've got the time to do it."

She led Jewell into the bathroom, immaculately done in ecru-and-white tile. She pushed a stool under Jewell and pulled out the tools of her trade: comb, brush, scissors.

Within seconds, the two women were as if old friends. Ma told Jewell funny stories about all her children, stories that highlighted a family clearly devoted to one another and clearly pulled up from near-tragedy by hard work and resourcefulness. Jewell was so entertained that she didn't focus on the mirror—such a change from the stuffy salon she ordinarily went to, where preening and primping and contemptuous looks at the competition were the order of the day.

So when Ma began to sweep up the platinum locks on the floor, Jewell was shocked and fascinated at what she saw.

"You know, you were really meant to be a brunette," Ma said. "Blond made you look hard as nails. But your natural hair color, such a pretty shade, like a cup of café au lait, really brings out your eyes. And short hair's good for you, you have such delicate features."

Jewell stared a few moments longer, realizing she was seeing herself for the first time. Before, she had only been a clone of every other Mississippi Delta debutante. Now she was Jewell Whittington, just herself. But a self that was deeply feminine, almost impish and warmer than she had ever imagined.

She wondered how often people had been intimidated by her looks, intimidated into thinking of her as cold and spoiled and full of herself. And maybe she had acted that way—reinforcing and being reinforced into a role that wasn't natural to her.

She pulled the Chanel double-C earrings from her ears.

"You're right," Ma said. "Too chunky. You need something scaled more to your petite size. Come on upstairs, I've got something you might like."

Jewell followed her up the polished stairway to the light, airy bedroom. Ma opened up a pine jewelry box on the antique vanity.

"Here's something that'll look good on you," she said, holding out a pair of delicate garnet earrings.

"They're beautiful, but I couldn't," Jewell said.

"Oh, Jewell, you have to learn," Ma warned. "You never really own anything—not jewelry, not houses and certainly not money. You just borrow it while you pass through this life. I borrowed those earrings from my sister, and someone will borrow them from you when the time is right."

"I'm very honored," Jewell said, and she put them on.

"Perfect," Ma said. "Now, let's go find my boy."

Jewell lingered at the vanity's mirror for one moment longer, still unsettled by her own image. And yet, she realized that, even as different as she looked now, she was more at home with herself than she had ever been.

Yes, this was her hair, with a simple pixielike cut—no peroxide, no intricate style held together with pins, spray and a prayer. This was her face, softly featured with luminous indigo-colored eyes, tea rose cheeks and pale pink mouth—no black eyeliner, no contouring foundation, and no Paloma Picasso fuchsia lipstick.

A funny thought popped into her head—she liked herself now. And she loved— She stopped herself, realizing how dangerous her thoughts were becoming.

She joined Ma and Clay in what appeared to be a library, judging by the books stacked everywhere. Then Jewell noted the twin bed and the pictures of family and realized this was the room Clay grew up in.

But something was terribly wrong.

Clay sat at a desk pushed up against a twin bed, staring at an official-looking document in front of him. He didn't look up when she entered the room. Ma sat on the bed staring at her hands. Gone was the warm, maternal friend—replaced with a woman whose face showed her age and the trials of her life.

"What's the matter?" Jewell asked.

"I just talked to my banker," Clay said. "The mortgage on the house is being called in."

"How can that be?" Jewell asked, sitting on the bed next to Ma. She held a comforting hand out to the older woman, and Ma took it.

"Ma got a letter yesterday, demanding payment of the mortgage in its entirety. I assumed when I read it that there was some sort of clerical error. It couldn't be."

"And?" Jewell choked.

"They're calling it in. My banker, Joseph Eastman, says he got a directive from the president of the bank. This has become too risky of a neighborhood."

"Is not," Ma said contentiously. "The neighborhood is just as bad as it was when I moved in here with all you kids. It's always been the wrong side of the tracks and it always will be. Hasn't bothered the bank before."

Clay shook his head. "Part of the terms of getting a mortgage to buy the house was that the bank could call it all in at any time," Clay said.

"So what are you going to do?" Jewell asked.

"We gotta get forty thousand dollars," Ma said.

"Call up your other children," Jewell suggested. "Surely the doctor or the lawyer or even the college professor could help out. Maybe even Al has enough money."

"No," Clay said decisively. "Paul is only six months out of medical school—he's a resident at

Vanderbilt and is barely making ends meet. If this happened three years from now, he could help out, but now it's impossible. As for Melanie, she works for legal services in Houston—she does a lot of good, but she doesn't make a lot of money. Andrea's just a first-year assistant professor. She's probably making less money than I used to give her for an allowance.''

"And Alice just had a baby," Ma said. "She doesn't have any extra money."

"What about Al?" Jewell asked.

"He's got bills to pay and he doesn't need me coming to him for help," Ma said firmly.

"That just leaves Clay," Jewell said, not saying the next thought that popped into her head—circumstances always seemed to leave Clay in charge of fighting off disaster.

"Do you have the money?" Ma asked fearfully.

He shook his head. "I have some of it, but not all," he admitted. "But I promise you, Ma, you're not going to lose the house."

Ma brightened considerably. "I know when my Clay tells me everything's going to work out, it will."

Clay looked up tiredly, and Jewell knew that his mother's words only seemed to add more pressure on him.

"Hey, did Ma do your hair?" he asked.

Jewell blushed and nodded.

"Looks nice," he said in an absent sort of way, and yet, he stared at her for several minutes until she grew uncomfortable under his scrutiny. She knew he was torn. Torn between wanting to dive right into the work of saving his mother's house and wanting to let his eyes linger.

"Let's get going," he said abruptly. "Ma, don't worry about this."

He held aloft the damning letter, and Jewell noticed tears welling in Ma's face.

"I'm counting on you, Clay," she said. "I don't mean to, and I never should have leaned on you as much as I did when you were growing up. But you always know what to do. Don't let them take this house away from me, Clay."

"I won't, Ma."

ON THE DRIVE HOME, Clay was quiet and grim, and Jewell knew enough to not press him. When they reached the gas station, she followed him into the stairwell leading to the apartment. He reached down to pick up the mail—a few catalogs, a couple of envelopes to "resident," and then he picked up a blue envelope Jewell recognized as the bank's stationery.

Without opening it, he ripped it into several pieces and threw the pieces to the ground.

"Why'd you do that?" she asked.

"Because I already know what's in there," he said. "I didn't say anything at Ma's house because I didn't want her to worry about me, but the Smiths have rejected my offer to buy the four gas stations."

"You were going to buy the gas stations?" Jewell asked, disbelieving. How could Clay afford it?

"Yeah, I had saved the money for a down payment and a business plan for continuing payments. We had been negotiating the price for months. I had given them my best offer, one that would have stretched me to my absolute limit but which I thought was a fair price. There's no way I can go higher—I've lost my chance,'' Clay said, bolting upstairs.

Jewell hurried to catch up with him. He shoved open the door to the apartment and gave Samson and Delilah only cursory pats on the head. The dogs whimpered and leapt up onto the bed.

"So what do they want?" Jewell said.

"They want more cash up front," Clay said, banging open the cabinet over the sink. "I wanted to pay off the business gradually. I had some money set aside, but not nearly as much as they want. And now I'm going to have to use that money to save Ma's house. So it doesn't matter. None of it matters. I'm finished."

He rummaged around some bottles and pulled out a fifth of whiskey. Jewell had never seen him drink anything stronger than beer—she knew he wasn't a drinking man. He opened the seal, pulled two jelly glasses out of the dishwasher and poured a fingerful in each.

"I've lost everything," he said bitterly, handing her one of the glasses. "I've lost my chance to be in business for myself and, while I might be able to save my Ma's house if I hustle, I'll never be able to put aside the money I think is necessary to ensure a pension for her. I'll always be playing catch-up, paying each month's bills as they come, never getting ahead, never building something for myself, something for my future, something for any children I might have. All I can give them now is this."

He held his glass aloft and surveyed the apartment—its cheery look now seemed cramped and faded.

He drank the whiskey and put the empty glass in the sink.

"The worst of it is, I've lost . . ."

"What?"

"I've lost you."

"Oh, Clay, no, you haven't. . . ." she cried out, putting her glass on the counter and rushing to his arms.

Even as she flung her arms around his neck, he pushed her gently away, holding her wrists to her sides.

"I have," he insisted. "You and I, we haven't got a future together. You're going back to your world, and I'm going to stay right where I am. We can have a one-night stand. Hell, we can play out our fantasies in bed right up until the day you walk out that door to go back to Pontchartreaux. A two-week stand, a month-long stand. But there isn't any future to it anymore."

"Why not? If I got my dad's money, you can pay off your Ma's house, put together a pension fund for her and buy all the gas stations in the state if you want."

He shook his head. "Jewell, I'm a man and I'm not going to be kept. I believe in old-fashioned things, like a man supporting his family. I have nothing, absolutely nothing, to offer you. And I have nothing to offer any child we would have, and that's completely unacceptable."

Jewell reared her head up, feeling a mixture of desperation and indignation.

"Clay, that's just plain sexist. If I have the money, what difference should it make?"

"All the difference in the world."

"But I know plenty of women who've married men with less money. Mindy, who had her debut at the same time I did, married a guy from Italy. All he had was a title, a dreamy accent and a lot of bills. Mindy is happy as a clam because now everyone's supposed to refer to her as a viscountess—but I never do."

"And do you respect him just as much as you would if it were the other way around? If Mindy were poor and the viscount were supporting her?"

Jewell paused and got ready to say "of course." But she hesitated too long.

"There's your answer," Clay said flatly. "And do they have kids?"

"Yes, they do. A little boy. Benjamin's six months now, sweet as can be."

"And where's he going to go to school?"

"Mindy's father is already paying for a nurse and says he'll pay for Ben to go to parochial school."

"And does the viscount want Benjamin in parochial school? Does he like the nurse who's taking care of his child."

"I don't know. I'm not sure that he had an opinion one way or another."

"Jewell, you're not sure if he had an opinion that it would matter. Sounds like Mindy's father calls the shots. I'm not going to be in the viscount's position."

"Well, what if I gave up trying to get my dad's money back?" Jewell asked desperately.

"Would you really do that? Knowing there really was some kind of fraud? Knowing you had been robbed, as surely as if you had been mugged on the street? Would you walk away from everything without trying to hang on to both me and the money? After all, it's your birthright," he finished bitterly.

Again, she hesitated. Would she really have to give up everything in order to be with Clay? Should she? After all, he had never said he loved her, hadn't asked her for her hand.

"I knew you were smart," Clay said, taking her hesitation for the answer he was looking for. "You're too smart to let somebody take from you what is rightfully yours."

"If you really believe that, what do we have left?"

With a groan, he pulled her into his arms, and Jewell nearly cried out with relief and happiness at his touch.

"We have tonight and we have until you go home, home to Pontchartreaux."

Jewell searched his eyes, looking for the amber softness that she could use to persuade him. But his eyes were hard and flat. She knew she had lost him, though they wouldn't actually part until much later.

She closed her eyes against the truth, but then realized there was something, something small, that she could do so that she'd always know that a part of their relationship would always live.

She was just a short-term affair for him.

She wasn't the woman he was thinking of when he imagined his future wife and children.

And she knew she could not persuade him otherwise.

How terrible it was that she was so far in, so far gone over him, so deeply in love, that she wouldn't leave in indignation tonight.

"Clay, I want to make you a deal," she said. "You help me get my money back . . ."

"Of course I'll do that, honey."

"Listen, I mean to make you a deal. You help me get the money back, and I promise to pay off your mother's house, put aside some money for her and I'll buy the gas stations from the Smiths."

He looked at her, and in that moment, Jewell knew she had sealed the terms of their relationship. He understood that she was surrendering to its temporary nature.

He would help her, all right, and she would be happy to give money to Ma, to starting up a business for him.

But she also knew that he would then be nothing more than a dear friend. He had supported his father's children through adversity and expected nothing less of himself for when he married and started his own family. But he could accept help, from a friend and not a lover, and he considered her offer for many minutes.

She couldn't tell if there was relief or despair in his eyes.

"All right," he said at last.

Jewell smiled tentatively and he responded.

They were past talking of banks and bankers, of riches and of their divergent futures.

They had this night.

It was all they had.

"For tonight," Clay said, nuzzling her neckline. "Let's talk about this haircut."

Jewell gasped at his soft kisses and fell again under the hypnotic spell of his sex, leaving reason and doubt and expectation behind.

"What about it?" she murmured as a lazy smile spread across her face.

"I like it. It leaves your neck so...exposed."

He kissed the tender skin at the nape of her neck, and Jewell forgot that they didn't have a future, that they barely had a past. All she could think of was the glorious present as he swung her up into his arms and carried her to the bed.

# Chapter Nine

He made love tenderly, caressing every inch of her as if he were trying to memorize her every feature. The baroque curve of her hairline, the mole above her left breast, the triangle of downy hair at her sex. He knew he would remember forever—and memory would have to be enough.

Far away, where the lights twinkled on lawn parties, where women laughed breathlessly and men stood stiffly in dinner jackets was where she belonged. Far away in ways so much more compelling than mere miles.

As he entered her, he held himself apart from her body in order to gain more control over himself. He wanted this to last as long as it could. His maleness stirred and then stilled, and then he thrust long and slow into her.

Remember, he told himself.

Remember this.

The feel of her warm and sleek caress of his sex.

And he would remember.

But while there was bittersweet longing, an intimacy was missing from their lovemaking—an intimacy that had been there only twenty-four hours before.

Ah, how time can destroy a man. Then, he had thought he had something to offer her, that she was no heiress and he no failure.

But now he had nothing to offer her. He was tied to support his mother—at least until his younger siblings got their footings and even then, he felt a protectiveness toward them that he knew would make him hesitate to ask for their help anytime. And now he had no chance of buying the business beneath his feet— one that he had slaved for as a working man for years, with no other goal than to someday own it. To work for another man, to see another man reap the profits of his hard labor, would be a bitter pill. But one he must swallow because he could not leave the delta while his mother lived and depended on him.

With these worries pushed to the back of his brain, he focused on Jewell, thinking that perhaps his blessing was merely that he could have her for the moment, that this treasure was as much as any man could ask for. Any man who had been born to poverty as he had been.

So he memorized the contours of his fleeting gift— kissing each inch of flesh to imprint her taste upon him, letting her scent dominate him as her own excitement rose, caressing each ruby-tipped breast so that later, his own fingers would remember, and thrusting into her with long, deep strokes that communicated to him every bit of her innocent response.

But he avoided her eyes, unable to meet her gaze as his own heart broke. She would try to persuade him, try to tell him that her money could support them both, that he didn't need to work.

But she didn't understand what he needed to do to be a man. And if he wasn't a real man, she would someday know it, and her love for him, her respect for him as a man, would be destroyed.

So would her love, if this was love.

When they came together, bound by physical upheaval and release, he lingered only briefly inside her.

And then pulled out of her and lay down on his bed to stare at the ceiling and curse the fates that made them who they were.

But Clay hadn't overcome the fortune he'd been given at twelve by giving in to lingering bitterness and thoughts of regret.

By the time Jewell's breath stilled and her heartbeat returned to normal, he had turned away from a future that had never really existed. He kissed her forehead and smoothed her hair until she slept, and when he slipped out of bed to go out into the night, she didn't even stir.

"THAT WAS CHERISE'S," Jewell said to Clay as he walked into the office to fill out a work order.

He wiped his hands on a paper towel and looked at her questioningly.

"Cherise's is the dress shop where I used to buy things off the rack," Jewell explained. "I went in there right after my dad's funeral, and they said they didn't have any job openings. But they do now."

"What would you do?" Clay asked, careful not to let his emotions show. He didn't want her to leave, but it would happen—maybe sooner was better than later.

"Oh, nothing much," Jewell said coolly, puzzled and hurt by the fact that Clay didn't immediately ask her to stay. "I would be like a hostess. Not really a saleswoman. Cherise was clear that I wouldn't have to ring up purchases or take inventory or do anything like that—just sort of be there in the store and wear the clothes and show customers how to dress."

"Doesn't sound like much work to me," Clay commented.

Jewell felt stung. "Well, it would pay a lot more than I'm getting here, and I'd have an unlimited clothing allowance."

Clay's eyes narrowed. "Doesn't that sound a little too good to be true?" he asked. "I mean, think about our business—I mean, the Smiths' business. Do you imagine they could hire somebody to park a Jaguar out by the gas pumps and tell people their own cars don't look good enough?"

Jewell's mind worked rapidly. "You're right. It sounds pretty weird. But she's the one making the business decisions. It's actually the second job offer I've gotten this morning."

"Really?"

"Yeah, my old hairdresser called and..."

"Let me guess. More money. No work to do."

"Well, I'd be answering questions about beauty, making women feel comfortable..."

"How? Putting pillows behind their heads? Look out there in the parking lot. Do you think this business could survive if there was somebody out there fluffing pillows underneath our customers' heads?"

"Look, stop being so hostile to my working. These are good jobs, paying lots..."

"They're not good jobs. They're make-work jobs. They don't add anything to the business."

"Cherise said I could add a touch of class to her operation."

Clay chose his words carefully. "Of course you can. But you could have done that three weeks ago. Why now?"

"What do you mean, why now?"

"Why is she offering you a cushy job that doesn't add anything to her bottom line when three weeks ago she blew you off rather effectively?"

"You're just upset because . . ."

"I did a lot of thinking after you went to sleep."

The words startled her.

She hid it well, as well as a woman could, but Clay recognized the fleeting pain that crossed her face. He had been careful rising from their bed and he had been certain she was asleep. When he'd returned, her eyelashes, soft and dark and thick, hadn't moved.

But no woman likes to think of a man getting up alone after lovemaking.

He had needed the time to think, to drive his motorcycle as fast as the law allowed and then some, to talk to the solitary moon. She couldn't be part of that because what he needed to do was resign himself to losing her.

He could—no, would—someday overcome the odds again and make a success of himself. He would give his mother the economic security that was her due, he would shepherd his younger siblings to full independence and he would buy his own business. Not the Smiths'. But still, he had no doubt he would succeed. Someday.

But he would never, ever have the chance at making Jewell his own. That chance had been his only briefly and now it was gone. And by the time he was in a position to ask for her, she would belong to another man and have another man's baby.

And so he wanted to reach out and touch her cheek. Wanted to reassure her that when she opened her body to him, he kept her love as precious as diamonds.

But it wouldn't be fair to do that—wouldn't be fair to either of them when they both knew that this relationship was quickly approaching its dead end.

"Thinking?" Jewell asked quietly. "About what? About us?"

"There is no us," he said gently, as gently as he could.

She swallowed and tilted her chin upward. "While you've been thinking, I should tell you I've received a phone call from Winfield," Jewell said as they both watched his hand reach up to touch her and then fall limply to his side. "Winfield wants to get back together. He said he was sorry that he gave in to his family. I told him it was too late."

"Shouldn't have done that," Clay said, though the words cut into him as effectively as any knife would.

"Why not?" Jewell asked, her eyes sparkling with challenge.

"He's a good guy," Clay said, trying his best to keep the bitterness and grief from his voice. And trying to lie with as much conviction as he could muster. "He'll give you a nice life. Any man can make a mistake. He made his, being torn between his family and the woman he loves and making the wrong choice. I think you should give him a second chance."

Jewell flushed as deeply red as if he had slapped her.

They stared at each other for several minutes, and then Jewell looked away, her gaze skittering across the counter between them.

"You're looking forward to our parting," she said.

He walked around the counter and put his arms on her shoulders. His head dipped, and he rested his cheek against her head.

"I'm sorry, Jewell," he said. "It's hard knowing it's coming. I can't stand the idea of losing you."

"But you don't have to!" she wailed, turning around to face him. "It's only you who's making up this idea that we have to break up. I would stay with you if you would just ask."

"Stay with me when you're working at a hostess job at Cherise's or, better yet, when you've returned to Pontchartreaux? Stay with me when Winfield or any other man can offer you the world? Stay with me when I'm going to be deeply in debt for years and years?"

Jewell flung her arms around him. At first, he couldn't respond, could just hold himself back, the part of him that had always held himself back from love, that always held back from wanting, yearning, desiring anything or anyone for himself. But then something welled within him, as compelling as the Mississippi itself, and he held her to him. As tightly as he ever could—not now motivated by lust or by the sheer pleasure of her body or the sheer relief from loneliness. Now motivated by love.

For it was love he felt for her. Doomed and improbable as it was. He had never imagined for himself a woman to love, but without Jewell there would be a hole in his life.

Though they had not been together more than three weeks, he still could sense the Christmases and New Year's Eves and Fourths of July without Jewell. He could sense the blank spot in his life where their children would have been. He could smell the lack of her perfume, could hear the quiet of music shut off because there wasn't Jewell to dance with him.

"This is what they want," Jewell said. "This is what they want."

"What do you mean? Who do you mean, 'they'?"

"They want us to break apart," Jewell said with growing conviction. "They want us to break apart. They want me to go back to Winfield, or even more deviously, they want you to push me toward Winfield. They want you to be penniless, they want me to go back to being a frivolous, spoiled child."

"You mean the fates?"

"No. The bank."

He held her away from himself and studied her face. "What are you talking about?"

"Don't you see it? I think it's as plain as day. Hear me out. I know you think this is crazy, but I think the bank coming after your mom's house and the Smiths' rejecting your offer is related."

"Sure," Clay said slowly. "It's related in that both things are financial disasters for me."

Jewell smiled. "And the old Jewell would have immediately decided to dump you," Jewell said triumphantly. "After all, you can't buy me a bauble out of the Tiffany's catalog now."

"Thanks a lot."

"No, you don't understand. I've changed. I'm not that person anymore. But the bank doesn't know it."

"Why does the bank care? And what bauble are you thinking of anyhow?"

"Be serious. Let me finish. The old Jewell would have jumped at the chance to get an easy job, to get her fiancé back, to go back to safety and security and ease. But now I'm not so sure. Now I can recognize, with a little help, when a job is not really a job. I know when work is really work."

"Like running the cash register at a gas station?" he challenged.

"Yeah, that's important because it helps people, and the gas station isn't going to run without it. You're absolutely right that sitting at Cherise's filing my nails and telling a woman that an outfit looks divine on her isn't real work. But the old Jewell couldn't have been persuaded of that. You know, the old Jewell wouldn't have even cared."

"So what's the point?"

"The point is somebody's trying to make us break up. And if I were still the woman I was three weeks ago, they would have succeeded."

"But why would they want to break us up?"

"Because they know that, between the two of us, we'll uncover all the secrets about my father's will."

Clay shook his head, disbelieving.

Then he looked at her closely. "Does that lawyer Thomas Fogerty work for the bank?"

"He's on the board of directors."

"Jewell, you might just be on to something."

"I DON'T HAVE a good feeling about this," Clay said. "I think you should have stayed at home."

"Not on your life," Jewell whispered.

"Aren't you worried about breaking a nail?" Clay growled.

"These days I don't."

"All right, let me help you up. Which window is supposed to be open?"

"The latch on the window to my bedroom has never worked right."

In the dark, Jewell accepted his strong grip as he pulled her up to the roof of the sun porch and they contemplated the climb to the second-story window.

"And you say Michael's not going to be home?" Clay said.

"Absolutely. I called the house at ten-thirty and pretended to be the daughter of a friend of his mother's. I disguised my voice and made my suggestion for drinks as alluring as I could. It's ten forty-five now. Supposedly, he was meeting me at ten-thirty at L'Hermitage. It'll take him a while to catch on that no one's coming. Meanwhile, he'll have a few drinks.... By the way, I went to pay L'Hermitage what I owed them, and they said you'd already taken care of it."

"I don't want to talk about it," Clay said curtly.

"Fine. But let me say thanks. If I had been having dinner with me three weeks ago, I don't think I would have wanted to pay for the privilege."

"It was always a privilege," Clay said lightly.

They stood side by side on the roof of the sun porch and surveyed the climb to the second-story bedroom window.

"Are you sure?" Clay whispered.

"Absolutely. My dad kept his most secret papers in the safe in his study. If there is a real will, it's going to be there. And if we find the real will, then we have something to take the place of the fraudulent will. We might also get some clues about who made up the phony will."

"Then let's go," Clay said.

He scaled the brick facade and pulled himself up to the second-story window, reaching with one hand to slide the pane open. Then, biceps bulging as if muscle might burst from the tanned skin, he hoisted himself up and into the room.

He reached back out the window to help Jewell up.

"Last chance to just let me do this," he whispered.

"No, you don't know how to open the safe."

She reached to the familiar wall and flicked on the light. A sparkling chandelier splattered crystalline light over the muslin-canopied bed, the French Provincial furniture and the pale pink Aubusson rug. Clay turned the light off.

"Don't want to do that," he warned. "We don't know who can see us from the street."

"The road's a half-mile away."

"But this chandelier of yours could be used by NASA to guide rockets home."

"Oh, yeah, I guess you're right," Jewell said. She felt a shiver go up her spine. For the first time, she really understood that they were breaking the law. Breaking into a house that wasn't, as the law stood, hers. Worse, they were intruding on Michael's territory—and if he was slime enough to forge his own father's will, he probably was slime enough to hurt them if he found them here.

Clay followed her in darkness down the wide hall-way lined with nineteenth-century busts of previous Whittington heirs. She opened the door to the study and felt Clay slip in ahead of her. He flicked on a small flashlight.

"Know where it is?" Clay asked.

"Yeah. What's that sound?"

They both froze, and Clay flicked off the flashlight.

"It's just the wind," Clay whispered. "The willow tree is scraping back and forth across the window."

"No, it's something else," Jewell said doggedly. "It's footsteps."

"Isn't your brother supposed to be out at L'Hermitage?"

"Yeah, he's there. Or, at least, he was there ten minutes ago. I called the bar and asked them to check. But I'm still scared."

"You've been watching too many mystery movies. Come on. We've got a job to do—let's just do it. I don't appreciate breaking and entering as much as you do. I'm only doing this because you told me you were coming here on your own if I didn't."

He flashed the light over the wall, briefly illuminating the black oak desk and plush, matching upholstered armchairs.

"There!" Jewell declared. "The picture over the desk."

He lit the black-and-white landscape scene framed in baroque gold.

"It's Renoir," Jewell said proudly.

"Renoir woodcut, possibly from his days as a student," Clay said. "This same woodcut probably has two hundred companions, some in better condition than others."

"How'd you know that?"

"Hey, I read. Probably as much as you do. Now, get the safe open."

Jewell slid behind the desk and carefully pulled the woodcut from the two hooks that held it to wires hanging from the crown molding at the ceiling. Clay took the woodcut from her.

"It's beautiful," he said. "It's a great honor to have a piece of real artwork. Something beautiful, something real."

"It's yours," Jewell said, realizing that for all the original Renoirs, Picassos and Monets that graced her house, she'd never really thought about them.

"Thanks but no."

She didn't see the fleeting pain on his face that her reminder of status caused. Instead, she concentrated on the small dial on the wall.

"Do you know the combination?" Clay asked.

"Do you think I would have come all the way out here if I didn't?" Jewell parried. She frowned. "It's a combination of my birthday and my mother's birthday—but I'm having a little trouble."

"Here, let me help."

He slid up close to her, handing her the flashlight. He worked for several minutes, running through the combination as she whispered the numbers, lifting the latch only to have it catch.

"I once had a locker at school that was real touchy, hard to get open," Clay said.

"So what did you do?"

"Dropped out of school."

"Don't joke around, Clay. I'm awfully scared of what might happen if my brother..."

"Here," Clay said. "Stop worrying so much."

He flicked open the safe and pulled out a long, thin, gray metal box.

"This what you're looking for?" he asked.

"Yeah, put it on the desk and we'll go through it."

Clay shook his head. "Not a good idea. Just dump everything into your tote. I don't relish the thought of meeting up with your brother any more than you do, and every second counts. You sure your brother doesn't know about this safe?"

"I know he doesn't. My father told me this was his secret."

"But you were told about it."

"But Michael was different. He was never here."

She tipped the gray metal box on its side over her tote. Papers, letters, document envelopes, even a diamond bracelet slid into the fake patent-leather pouch.

"Look at this," Jewell said, pulling a diamond solitaire ring from the pile in her bag. "This was my mother's engagement ring."

Clay peered at it. "Looks pretty small for you. Looks normal sized. I would have expected something bigger from the Whittingtons."

"Oh, no, my father was quite poor when he was young. I mean, he had the Whittington house and that had been paid for years before, but the Whittingtons lost a lot of money after the War Between the States and even more money during the Depression. My father grew up in this big old house eating greens and grits like everybody else. His first wife, Michael's mother, got fooled that way—thought because he had a big house he had some money. And she was wrong."

"Until he got rich."

"Until he figured out a new system for growing cotton and soybeans more efficiently. Turned everything around. But that was long after he had divorced his first wife and married my mother. Then he replaced my mother's engagement ring with something much bigger. I never even saw this ring on my mother's hand."

"Too bad. Might have taught you something about hard work."

Jewell shook her head.

"I probably would have grown up just as spoiled as ever," she said ruefully. "I've given it a lot of thought and I think my father loved me so much that he wanted to make sure I never suffered, never had to work hard, never faced disappointment or trouble. And that just doesn't train a person for the real world."

She slid the empty metal box into the safe and closed the safe door over it. Clay admired the Renoir woodcut for a bare moment more before he slipped it into its hooks. He steadied the painting and looked at Jewell.

"Ready?"

She shook her head, eyes widened. "Don't you hear something?"

"No."

"No, stop. Listen. I'm sure I've heard something."

"Jewell, you're imagining things. I knew we shouldn't have watched that horror movie last night."

"Shh. Listen."

"You listen. It's dark and creepy and we're committing a felony. Maybe if we did this for a living, we would be a little more used to..."

Suddenly, from behind the door to the hallway, worked the slide of a 12-gauge shotgun. Jewell gulped and instinctively leaned closer to Clay.

She didn't even say "I told you so."

"Oh, damn," Clay whispered. "Maybe you did hear something."

"What are we going to do?" Jewell whispered.

"You go for the back stairs," he hissed.

"How do you know about the back stairs?"

"Because those stairs are for servants. And anytime I've ever been in this house, I've been a servant."

He swiftly moved to the door, grabbing a marble bust of General Robert E. Lee from the side table.

"No, Clay, that's an original Remington!" Jewell cried out.

The door flung open, a gunshot burst into the study and the chandelier dropped to the floor, sending a spray of broken crystal into the air. Clay leapt toward the intruder, dropping the Robert E. Lee bust unharmed to the floor.

Jewell screamed as her brother and Clay fell to the carpet, arms and legs grappling for purchase, the shotgun beneath them, the heavy sculpture rolled between them.

"Get the hell out of here!" Clay ordered her.

She stood rooted to the spot, looking desperately around the room for something heavy, something big, something really...

She grabbed the Robert E. Lee bust as the two men rolled away from her. Holding it aloft for maximum force, she dropped it on top of them, certain that her brother, who was now on top of Clay, would be stunned into powerlessness.

Instead, the bust grazed Clay on the shoulder.

And missed Michael completely.

So much for Robert E. Lee.

"Jewell, would you just get out of here! You've got to get those papers out of here."

"What papers?" Michael grunted, pulling away from Clay.

Clay pounced, gaining the advantage and yanking Michael up from the carpet to punch him soundly on his upper lip. Michael looked at Clay, then at Jewell, stunned.

And then he fell back, unconscious, to the carpet.

"Jewell, move it!" Clay ordered, leaping up. "Grab your bag and let's run."

But a play of light across the ceiling caught his eye, blue-and-red arcs of light. A dog barked ferociously at a distance, but as it approached, it got louder and louder. The sound of radio transmissions filtered through the shouts of men on the front lawn. The doorbell rang, an incongruously elegant and sedate sound that suggested genteel and sedate hospitality.

"The police! Jewell, go down those back stairs."

"What about you? Aren't they going to arrest you?"

"Sure they will. And I hope to God that paperwork turns out to be worth it. Bail me out as soon as you can—or, at least, visit me in prison from time to time," he finished with a brave wink.

He kissed her on the forehead and firmly pushed her toward the narrow door that led to the stairs.

"Go!" he ordered.

Jewell paused and then obeyed just as the front door burst open and three blue-uniformed sheriff's officers, guns drawn, spread out across the front foyer.

# Chapter Ten

Dear Michael,
I am appalled that you would use the safety of
your own half sister, Jewell, as a bargaining chip
to extort more money from me. Yet I am suffi-
ciently convinced of the seriousness of your threat
that I enclose a money order in the amount of ten
thousand dollars made out to the New Hope
Shelter for the Homeless. You are a con man, a
scam artist and worse, and it is only the fact that
you are my flesh and blood that stops me from
calling the police—although sometimes I wonder
if it would be the best thing for you. I feel a bur-
den of guilt for whatever I have done to create
and mold you into the monster you are today.

Still, I warn you that if you lay a hand on Jewell, my heart will harden against you and I will
not hesitate to use any resources in my possession to see justice done.

Jewell folded the carbon paper and replaced it,
along with dozens of similar letters, into a large manila envelope. Receipts for nearly fifty money orders

made out to her half brother were in a separate envelope.

The last letter had been written two days before her father's heart attack. There was no doubt in Jewell's mind that she now had sufficient proof that her father's will—leaving everything to her half brother and the New Hope shelter—was simply another in a series of scams, frauds, forgeries and extortions.

Although the fraudulent will was definitely Michael's biggest effort, she wasn't sure how he had enlisted Thomas Fogerty's help.

While she felt sorry for Michael, who so clearly had felt great pain about being abandoned by his father in the course of his parents' divorce, she couldn't feel sorry for the man he had become. One who would do anything to satisfy his own self-interest.

He had made his own bed, chosen his own course in life, taking the path of easy money over hard work and initiative. Jewell had no doubt that her father would have paid for Michael to go to the finest universities, would have financed the start-up costs for any business Michael wanted to pursue, would have helped his son in any way possible. The earliest letters proved this—many a check, many a money order, was accompanied by a proud letter congratulating Michael on choosing to work hard or go back to school. These letters were the most poignant, and were inevitably followed by notes of outrage upon Charles's discovery that his son wasn't at school, wasn't working and had no intention of doing anything other than continuing his life of leisure.

She leaned back on the pillows of the bed, smelling Clay's lingering scent of lime and musk. She looked with revulsion at the other oversize envelope, which contained originals—letters from her half brother to her father. Reading each one had been horrifying as she watched the spreading tentacles of her half brother's scheme to take her father's fortune.

The phone rang, startling her out of her brooding thoughts. She got out of bed, stepped over Samson and Delilah, who were desultorily playing with a plastic duck, and picked up the extension in the kitchenette.

"Hello?"

"Hi, Jewell, it's Al. They just finished taking Clay's statement. He'll be coming home soon."

She felt a sudden pang of hurt. "I was going to come get him. But when he called me, he told me to wait. Said the police say they don't need my statement until tomorrow and that he wouldn't be getting out any time soon."

There was a long pause.

"Clay says you guys might be breaking up soon," Al said slowly. "So he didn't want to...impose by asking you to come down. I think he wants to be with his family now."

With his family?

The obvious point was that she wasn't part of that family.

"Oh, God," Jewell cried out, her heart beating faster. "Why would he think we were breaking up?"

"Jewell, you've got your own life to live. You're getting your home back, and when the legal stuff gets cleared up, you'll be a rich young woman again."

"But that won't happen for a while," Jewell said, grasping at straws. "Getting Michael out of my life will be hard. I've been reading this paperwork. He's pretty tenacious. It'll take a long time for lawyers to sort through this."

"Michael's already out of town," Al reassured her. "At the house, the police were going to charge Clay with assault and battery, but then Clay had a little chat with Michael before he bolted. I don't know what he said, but the police will be looking for him for a long time. Only Thomas Fogerty'll be left holding the bag—they've arrested him already, but it looks like he was blackmailed into participating in the scheme after your father's death. But don't worry about Michael. Clay took care of him."

"Wow."

"That's what I said. Clay's one tough guy. Uh, Jewell, he knows you guys don't have a future and you'll be moving out on him soon. I know you have your own life to live. But let me ask you, just as his younger brother, please be gentle with him. He's got a tender heart, a soft spot, and I don't think he even knows it."

"Of course I'll be gentle with him."

"I figured you would. But, you know, money screws things up just as much as it helps."

"I think you're right," Jewell said, thinking briefly about her brother. Michael was roughly the same age as Clay and had had advantages that Clay couldn't even imagine. How differently the two men had taken their fortunes. Clay had used every bit of energy he had to create a better life for those who depended on him. With hard work and resourcefulness and determination. And Michael had diverted his energy toward pleasure seeking and conscious avoidance of work or study.

All Clay had to do was say he loved her, and she would stay.

"That's not true," Al said, and Jewell realized that she had spoken her thoughts aloud. "You're a Whittington and you belong at Pontchartreaux. My brother doesn't belong there. And he knows it."

Jewell felt the sting of first tears against her eyes.

"Do you really think that's true?" she asked.

"I don't know you well enough to know for sure, but I know my brother, and where you're going, he doesn't belong."

"Maybe you're right."

She said goodbye to Al and, as Jewell hung up, she looked around the apartment. It was hard to believe that she had lived for nearly four weeks with Clay and two dogs in a room that wasn't much bigger than her dressing room at Pontchartreaux.

Boy, it would be different going home.

She scooped up the paperwork from the bed and put it in her tote. Then she noticed the tiny diamond ring that had been her mother's. She slipped it on her finger.

There were bigger jewels in the Whittington safe-deposit box—jewels that were all hers now. An emerald tennis bracelet. A necklace made of freshwater pearls and a four-carat ruby clasp. A diamond tiara that Jewell had worn at her debut ball, the same tiara that had graced the heads of Whittington women for generations and had been pawned and repossessed three times. A matching set of diamond-and-sapphire bracelet, necklace and drop earrings.

Still, the tiny diamond ring was pretty in its own way. Symbolizing the love that had created her, a love that had somehow survived and thrived through good times and bad—until death had taken her mother.

Maybe the ring would give her luck.

Because she needed luck—she had some delicate persuading to do.

Regardless of what Al said, she would try. Maybe Clay could be happy at Pontchartreaux. He'd be master of all the land he could see from the house. She'd let him do anything he wanted, pursue any goal he chose.

She knew a proper debutante shouldn't be the one doing the courting, but these were special circumstances.

Circumstances no proper debutante would get herself into in the first place.

With some optimism for her success, she put her wallet in her pocket and patted each dog goodbye and then she raced down the stairs to the sidewalk. The convenience store was the only thing that was open all night, but it would have to do. She had to create the right atmosphere, and if she didn't have a hundred-dollar bottle of champagne to help her, she'd settle for whatever the store had to offer.

"DON'T TURN ON THE LIGHT," Jewell ordered from behind the bathroom door.

Clay looked around the candlelit room. Fragrant votives scattered golden light over the walls and ceiling, creating a romantic atmosphere that made even Samson and Delilah look good.

"Uh, Jewell, I don't think is a very good idea," Clay said. "I think we need to talk."

The bathroom door swung open, as if of its own accord. Inside, more votives. Clay peered in and groaned.

Jewell lay in the tiny bathtub, bubbles covering her. A bottle of Spanish champagne chilled in a steel bucket. She held up a fluted glass.

"Would you pour?" she asked huskily.

Clay closed his eyes, willing his body to ignore the seductive swell of her breasts above the bubbles and the shadow of her sex beneath the water's surface.

"Jewell, this is a terrible idea," he said. "See, you're going back to that house, and I'm not going with you. And I think it'll just complicate matters if..."

He heard the wave of the water.

He opened his eyes. "Oh, Jewell, don't do this to me."

She was like Venus rising naked and glistening from the iridescent water. She did not cover her sex, and there wasn't enough hair on her head to modestly arrange to hide her breasts. The bubbles that had clung to her flesh slid down to the bubbly surface.

"Don't push me, Jewell, I won't be able to stop myself."

"I don't want you to stop," she said with a wicked smile. "That's the whole point."

She stepped delicately out of the tub and nearly, but not quite, touched him. She held her glass out to him, and when he took it, she walked out to the room.

Her not touching him was more provocative than if she had done the expected thing. If she had touched him, he would have taken her right there, against the door of the bathroom. It would have been a hot, quick possession. And then he would have been able to be done with her.

As it was, he felt the pressure of desire ratcheted up higher as she strolled to the bed, as she proudly— without a measure of false or coy modesty—looked over her shoulder to return his gaze.

He sighed and picked up the bottle of champagne and the extra glass. He poured two glasses to their brim and followed her to the side of the bed. She pulled the sheet down and spread out on the bed as provocatively as a cat.

"Jewell, why are you doing this?" he asked. "Do you want one final roll in the hay? Because that's all we have left."

His harsh words made her flinch, and she reached for the sheet to cover herself, but then she remembered that she had expected a little resentment, a little hostility.

She looked him straight in the eye. "Clay, I have a tiny favor to ask you."

"Oh, man, ever since the day I met you, you've been asking me favors," he said, trying desperately to depersonalize his feelings. "Our whole relationship has been one long favor."

She reached up to unbutton his jeans. He sighed as she released his sex—so hard, so very hard.

"All right, Jewell, ask away. You know I can't say no."

She knelt on the mattress, teasing him with champagne-flavored kisses on his neck and, as she ripped open the buttons on his shirt, he let his head drop backward in mortal ecstasy.

"Just tell me," he begged. "What's the damned favor?"

She pulled him down to the bed, his shirt clinging to his hot, clenched muscles with scented water from her flesh. He reached beneath her and found her sex, teasing instinctively until she was wet and slick and ready for him.

"Clay," she moaned as he slipped himself into her. "Clay, I just want to ask you for one last thing."

He was beyond listening, nearly beyond anything but the sensation of himself inside of her, possessing her a final, poignant time. His movements came more quickly, stronger and more confident.

As he thrust again and again, she went beyond reason to meet him. She knew this would happen, that her plan must account for passion and senselessness, and so she let go of her conscious mind and gave herself to pleasure, the pleasure that she hoped to have and hold. They both cried out, in that lush country, and then stilled. Clay lay on top of her, careful to balance his weight on his own elbows.

He looked down at her, his eyelids dark and heavy with sensual power.

"Now, what was that favor?" he asked suspiciously.

Jewell took a deep breath. It was harder than she had imagined.

"Clay, I want you to marry me."

He did a double take. "You want me to marry you when I don't have a damned thing to offer you?"

"You have yourself, and that's enough for me."

He rolled off of her and lay in the center of the bed, staring at the ceiling.

"Jewell, I love you so much that I'm awfully tempted."

"So marry me. The only thing that stands in our way is my money, and most people would think of that as a good thing. Clay, let me ask you a question— would you have married me if I never got back a dime of my father's money?"

"You bet I would have. I would have been the one doing the asking."

"If you were ready to marry me when I didn't have a dime to my name, why should my having several million make a difference?"

"You really think it won't?"

"No, it's not going to make any difference, except good ones. Wouldn't it be nice to pay off your mother's house and put aside some money for her?"

"Joe Eastman from the bank has already called and said that the bank isn't going to foreclose on the house. Thomas, acting on Michael's orders, put pressure on the bank to foreclose because they thought you'd break up with me and get out of town, out of their hair, if I was poor. Ma's house isn't going to be taken from her."

"But wouldn't it be nice to never worry about it again?"

"Yeah," Clay said cautiously.

"And if you wanted to own the Smiths' gas stations, you could."

"But it's your money."

"If we were married, it'd be our money."

Clay shook his head. "I don't want a penny."

"If we had children—"

"When we have children," Clay corrected.

Jewell smiled. "When we have children, lots of children, think of all the advantages we can give them, things you never had."

"But I don't want to spoil them."

"I'm not talking about doing that. I'm talking about letting them go to the best colleges, buying them the computers that are so essential these days, hiring tutors for them if they need extra help in school, buying them sports equipment when they need it."

Clay nodded. "Those things are important. I won't disagree with you."

"Besides, we did have an agreement saying I'd pay off your mom's house and buy the gas stations for you if you helped me recover my money. So it's only fair that you take the money. All I'm asking is that you take me, too."

"All right, all right, you win, you little vixen, I can never seem to say no to you."

He pulled her on top of him and kissed her—long and deep and languorously, with the quickened passion spent and a more sensuous hunger rising.

"Already?" Jewell giggled.

"All ready," Clay confirmed.

THE SUN SLIPPED through the lace curtains, bathing the eggshell walls with gold-and-amber light. Samson and Delilah, flopped together at the foot of the bed, stirred slightly and then groaned contentedly as they fell back to sleep. Clay shifted his feet to reclaim the warm spot beneath the two dogs' bodies. Jewell's eyes fluttered open, and while she didn't move because Clay's arms held her tight, she was wide-awake.

She had everything that could possibly make a woman happy.

The man she loved, a promise to wed—even if she blushed hot red just thinking how she had been the one to do the asking. And on top of all that, her birthright returned to her. She smiled like a satisfied cat.

Unbidden, plans unfolded in her head. A small but tasteful wedding at the Episcopalian chapel where her own parents had wed. She'd have to call Rev. Copland immediately. Her dress would have to be her mother's, and Jewell made a mental note to take the dress to the seamstress for some repair work on the beaded bodice. Clay could get a tuxedo in town.... Here she stopped herself.

Clay would rather marry quietly, very quietly. Probably in jeans and a work shirt if left to his own devices. And if she loved him, really loved him, how she married him should be less important than whether she married him.

So she shook her head to erase the images of a traditional wedding.

And yet, moments later, a sample menu was flitting through her head. *Escargots en croute*—snails in a pastry shell—for an appetizer. Perrier-Jouët champagne. Jewell wondered what would be better for the entrée—chicken or beef. Maybe a hundred people, yes, very small, in the ballroom at Pontchartreaux. One of the first things she'd have to do when she returned to the house would be to have the ballroom aired out and the tiles replaced underneath where the roof had leaked last summer.

She stretched and looked at her hands in front of her.

The tiny diamond of her mother's ring sparkled bravely.

What had Clay said about a two-hour engagement? About making a decision to marry and walking right over to the courthouse to get it done?

The tiny diamond, a promise of love everlasting, twinkled.

Oh, of course, a manicure. Pedicure, too, for that matter. Jewell also wondered if she should touch up her hair. Just a little blond. Highlights, really.

The telephone rang. Clay stirred but didn't wake. She slipped from his arms and got up to answer the phone by the kitchenette. She was surprised to hear from her "best" girlfriend.

"Mindy, such a pleasant surprise," she said coolly. Mindy had been "not at home," according to her housekeeper, every time Jewell had called in recent weeks.

"I'm so glad I finally got hold of you," Mindy exclaimed. "I was so worried! But I understand you'll be moving back to Pontchartreaux this morning, and I wanted to be the first to invite you over for dinner. Tonight. I mean, I'm sure your house will be in such disorder, you won't have a free moment to plan a meal, so do come over and join us."

"I, uh, I don't think..."

"Don't say no to me, Jewell. I've missed you so much."

"But you've been avoiding my phone calls for weeks now," Jewell said. "I got the impression you didn't want anything to do with me as long as . . ."

"Jewell Whittington! Such an idea. I'm mortally offended. Now, just come on over for dinner and put that silly notion out of your head. You should save your sassy attitude for somebody like Thomas Fogerty or your half brother. Although it's hard not to feel sorry for Thomas, because I understand Michael was blackmailing him with gambling debts Thomas had. I've never done a thing wrong to you, Jewell, I've just been out of town."

"All right, all right," Jewell said reluctantly. She looked over at the bed at Clay, who was stretching awake with all the sensuality of a lion. "But I'll be bringing a guest."

"A man?" Mindy asked naughtily.

"Yes, his name is Clay DeVries. We're getting married."

"Oh, Jewell, I'm so happy for you. DeVries? Name doesn't sound familiar . . . oh, wait!, is he a member of the DeVries of Cincinnati, the ones who own all those department stores?"

"I met him at Smith's gas station. He's worked there for ten years."

There was a long pause.

"Well, you're over twenty-one," Mindy said, trying to regain the conversational balance. "You can do what you want. We'll be looking forward to meeting him. Say seven?"

"Yeah, that'd be great," Jewell said.

"Jewell, I just want to tell you that I've missed you terribly," Mindy said, suddenly more serious.

"I've missed you, too," Jewell said impulsively.

She hung up the phone and walked back to the bed. Clay looked at her quizzically.

"We're having dinner at Mindy's house," she said. "Is that all right?"

Clay nodded. "Okay, but I can't make it at seven."

"Why not?"

"I have to close out the books."

"Can't you get somebody else…" Jewell started to say, and then she remembered how important Clay's work was to him, how important it would continue to be, and she had to accommodate him if they were to have any hope of a long and sweet relationship.

"I'll call Mindy back and tell her to expect us around eight-thirty."

Clay smiled, pleased at her effort. "Maybe this is going to work out," he said.

"I know it will," Jewell said, crawling into bed next to him.

AN HOUR LATER, they drove the pickup over to Pontchartreaux, letting Samson and Delilah ride in the back.

"Here it is," Jewell said as Clay pulled into the half-mile-long driveway. "Our new home."

"Sure looks a lot better in daylight, when we're not contemplating a break-in," Clay quipped.

As they came to a stop in front of the fountain, the front door burst open and Mia shot out.

"Oh, Miss Whittington!" she cried out. "I'm so glad you're home."

Jewell climbed out of the passenger's seat and gave Mia a big hug.

"Miss Whittington, you would not believe the inside of the house!" Mia exclaimed. "I tried to keep up after your brother, but he was such a mess, hell-bent on destroying—"

Mia stopped her diatribe long enough to watch Samson and Delilah trot into the open door—muddy footprints and all. Mia wrinkled her nose but gamely returned her attention to her mistress.

"Please call me Jewell from now on," she said. "'Miss Whittington' sounds too formal since I've known you all my life, and besides, I'm going to be changing my name soon anyhow."

She gestured toward Clay, who leaned against the hood of the pickup, his sunglasses dangling from his hand, his work uniform only slightly wrinkled from one last lovemaking before they had left the apartment.

"Oh, Clay," Mia said. "I've heard about how you've been so kind to Miss Whittington—I mean, Jewell. I'm sure she's going to be hiring you for all kinds of work. That pig of a half brother destroyed the tiles in the bathroom by running the water to overflowing, trampled through the rose beds without watching where he was going and—"

"No, you don't understand, Mia. Clay and I are getting married."

Mia's mouth flew open, but no sound came out. She stared at Clay, then at Jewell and then again at Clay, whose insouciant smile made her eyebrows jump.

"Married?" she asked Jewell in a bare whisper.

"Married," Jewell confirmed, amused that the normally unflappable housekeeper had at last been shocked.

Samson and Delilah reappeared. Samson with a small needlepoint pillow that had been made in the nineteenth century and was probably worth hundreds of dollars. Delilah yanked it from Samson's mouth and threw it up into the air. The pillow landed in the mud at Mia's feet. Before the horrified housekeeper could reach for it, Samson flung himself upon the pillow, growled and tore it to shreds as playfully and as certainly as if it were one of the squeeze toys that Clay bought for him.

Mia settled her chin firmly into a line of disapproval.

"My congratulations to the two of you," she said primly. "I will serve coffee in the breakfast room."

With great dignity, she picked up the shredded needlepoint and stuffing and marched back into the house. Samson and Delilah had abandoned their toy for a romp in the rose beds.

"How come she doesn't approve of you?" Jewell asked.

"Because no matter how low on the social ladder you are around here, you are always ahead of the DeVrieses," Clay said.

"I apologize for her behavior, then," Jewell said. "I'll talk to her about it."

"You'll do no such thing. I'm not a child. And respect isn't something you order—or have your wife order. I'd prefer to be like any other man and earn my respect. Even the respect of your housekeeper. She likes me well enough when I know my place. Don't do anything."

"Okay," Jewell said, coming over to put her arms around Clay. "I guess I'm going to have to learn how to do things around you. You're so independent."

"I wouldn't be a man if I was any other way."

"I love you, Clay. Just the way you are."

"Good, I love you, too," he said, kissing her tenderly on the forehead. "But I have a question."

"What?"

"If Mia disapproves of me this much, do you have any idea how your friends are going to react to me?"

Jewell pulled away, only to cover his face with reassuring kisses.

"Oh, Clay, you're so wrong if you think my friends are going to be snobs," she said at last. "One thing I know for sure is that all of my friends are going to love you from the moment they meet you."

# Chapter Eleven

*All of my friends are going to love you.*

Clay stared at the crystal glass in his hand, which was filled with a mint julep and sporting a dainty sprig of fresh mint. He would have rather had a Dixie longneck.

Or just a soda would be fine.

He shifted around on the wicker chair—imported as part of a six-piece set all the way from the French Indies—and worried that the crinkling sound meant the chair was going to collapse under his two-hundred-pound muscular weight. He couldn't get comfortable. It wasn't that kind of furniture. He had discovered in the past three weeks that rich people tended to own a lot of furniture that wasn't meant to be comfortable or used.

He tugged at his tie and closed his eyes.

*All of my friends are going to love you.*

"Hello, you must be Clay. I'm Winfield."

Clay opened his eyes to see beyond the outstretched hand.

So this was Winfield.

Red faced, as if even growing up in the Mississippi Delta he still hadn't gotten used to the sun. Blinking pale blue eyes that made him look like a quizzical rabbit. Clay reached to take the outstretched hand and then paused.

If he were meeting the man who had stolen his fiancée, he wouldn't shake hands.

He'd punch him.

And, as a matter of fact, Clay himself had thought it worthwhile to punch Winfield for breaking up with a woman when she was at her darkest hour.

But as he took Winfield's pale, manicured hand into his own large, callused one, he knew this spurned man didn't have any plans for retribution and that punching him wasn't worth it.

"Mind if I join you?" Winfield asked.

Clay shrugged a barely positive response, and Winfield sat on the settee.

"I wanted to meet you so I could express how delighted I am that Jewell has at last found happiness," Winfield said. "I just left her in the study with my sister, and Jewell is just chattering away like a parrot about plans for your wedding. She is so excited, and I'm sure it's going to be the event of the summer season."

Clay grunted and looked out onto the field where the gardener was directing the workers planting a new bed of wisteria. Clay thought with longing for the days when the sun was hot and he shucked off his shirt and the work was hard, real hard. He thought about the work and remembered how a drink of just plain old water tasted better than any of the champagne or cocktails he'd been drinking in the past three weeks as the new master of Pontchartreaux and as the social oddity of the Mississippi upper crust.

Winfield cleared his throat and Clay looked at him.

"I also wanted to extend an invitation to take you to the club this week," Winfield said. "Perhaps tomorrow, say, ten in the morning."

"The club?"

"Yes. It's right out on Jackson Boulevard," Winfield said, gesturing vaguely in a southerly direction.

"I know where it is."

"I thought we could play some golf."

"I don't know how."

"Jewell mentioned that. I thought I might take you out, show you how it's done. I'm sure you'd pick up the game in one morning, tops." He dropped his voice to a more confidential tone. "It's really how the men find time together. You know, the women have shopping and, uh, . . . ."

"Shopping," Clay supplied, thinking of Jewell's increasingly frequent trips.

Winfield laughed. "You're right. Shopping and shopping. Us guys have to stick together and we do it out on the golf course. I'd be delighted to sponsor you as a member, although, of course, the Whittingtons have had a family membership since the War Between the States. But Jewell mentioned that you like to do things on your own, so your own membership might make you feel more comfortable."

Clay ignored the clutch in his throat and the niggling annoyance at Jewell for talking to others about his personal thoughts and feelings. Still, if he was going to be part of this crowd for the rest of his life . . .

"Don't guys around here play football?"

"I played a little in high school," Winfield admitted, and then shook his head. "Clay, nobody plays after they've graduated. It's more a young man's sport."

"What about pool?"

"We call them billiards, and some men do play."

"How 'bout World Wrestling Federation matches?"

The look of horror on Winfield's face was priceless. It made the red on his face brighten into half a dozen splotches.

"Just joking," Clay said.

"Oh, of course. Making a joke. Ha. Rather funny. Well, let's get back to the issue of teaching you golf. An essential skill, you know."

Clay stared out at the garden, watching the workers bake in the sun, their muscles outlined against their clothes, their skin glistening with sweat.

"Winfield, let me ask you a question. Do you work?"

Winfield looked puzzled, and Clay resisted the urge to define *work.*

"Oh, of course, I know what you mean. I have an office in town. My father's law firm. Actually, my great-grandfather founded it right after the war."

"What do you do?"

"Well, I, uh, well, um, review contracts and trust matters for our clients. That sort of thing."

"When do you get in in the morning?"

"Midmorning, around ten."

"And when do you finish up?"

"Generally, sometime before four o'clock. And lunch is a rather substantial part of my business."

"Lunch?"

"Having lunch with businessmen, clients and other lawyers is how we network. Networking is very important. Perhaps the most important part of my day."

"How long do these lunches last?"

"Oh, maybe two, three hours."

"So we're talking about a total of four hours work, tops."

"I suppose."

"And it's your law firm."

"It's not really my law firm," Winfield said. "But if I'm going to inherit the firm, I'd better at least have some idea of what's going on. Don't you think?"

"Yeah, I guess so," Clay said vaguely, putting his glass on the marble-tiled floor and standing up. "Winfield, I've got to talk to Jewell."

"Sure, of course," Winfield said, and as Clay walked through the French doors to the sitting room, he called out, "Remember, we've got to get you out on the golf course. This week, if you can't make it tomorrow morning. My treat. Be sure to have Jewell pick you up a pair of golf shoes and some clubs."

Clay didn't hear those last words, but even if he had, he wouldn't have cared. He took the bridal staircase two steps at a time and burst into the study to find Jewell surrounded by her girlfriends. Travel brochures were spread out on the coffee table in front of them.

"Clay," she said breathlessly. "I was just looking at these—what would you think of a honeymoon in Majorca?"

He pulled her to her feet. "Jewell, we have to talk," he said. He ignored the suggestive leers of her friends.

"Clay, what on earth . . . ?"

He led her into the master bedroom and shut the door behind them.

"Clay, what is this about?"

"Did you get your nails done?"

Jewell looked down at her magenta-colored tips.

"Yes. They were looking pretty ragged."

"Tips?"

"Yeah."

"And you've put color in your hair?"

"Just highlights," Jewell said defensively. "Why are you asking me? You don't sound like you're about to hand out any compliments."

"You look fine, it's just, Jewell, I've got to go."

"You can't. We're having sixteen people for brunch. Guests are just now arriving."

"I'm going back to the gas station."

"You can go back in three hours, after they leave. Everyone will miss you otherwise—everyone's been dying to meet you."

"They met me last night."

"Oh, but that was a much larger crowd, over a hundred guests. Nobody had a chance to say more than a quick hello to anybody else."

She looked at the pained expression on Clay's face.

"Clay, this'll all die down after our wedding. Most women have a year-long engagement, and we've had to pack a year's worth of parties and get-togethers and showers into just a few weeks."

"Leave it all behind, Jewell—these people aren't really your friends. Where were they when you were broke?"

She felt the familiar ache of pain as she thought of those weeks.

"Sure, they weren't there for me in a pinch, but this is the group we're going to be associating with when we're married. It's the group I've grown up with all my life."

"You don't have to be friends with anybody who doesn't act like a friend."

"I don't have to carry a grudge against anybody, either."

"I'm not talking about carrying a grudge. I'm talking about remembering who really loves you."

"So what do you want me to do?"

He put his arms around her, and she felt the familiar rush of love and caring. It was always there, beating strong within her. But now it was tainted with guilt and with a dark pressure.

There were people congregating at the bottom of the stairs. Mia had let them in, but a proper hostess greeted her guests promptly. And the kitchen needed her attention. Just one more look-over at the dining-room table.

Why couldn't he see she was doing this for him? To make him more comfortable. To give him all that he had never had.

"I want you to come down to the courthouse with me right now," Clay said at her ear. "Let's marry now, today. And one other thing. I don't want to live here anymore."

"What? You want me to walk out on a house filled with guests and then, what, give up my home forever?"

"Yes, if you love me, you'll understand that anything else will destroy us. I feel like a trained monkey in this house. You think you're teaching me to be a 'gentleman' with fancy new suits, but all I want is my blue jeans. You think it's a treat for me to dine on lobster and caviar—when all I want is some simple fried chicken and mashed potatoes. And I can't get a decent, regular person's beer in this house—I keep getting handed cocktails with fancy garnishes. And a man has to work."

"I'm not stopping you," Jewell said coolly.

"Yes, you are. Every day there's some new party or fitting at the tailor or meeting with the bank officials or seeing your friends. Sometimes, I see so much of them that I wonder why they bother to go home in between meals."

"All of my friends love you."

"That's exactly what worries me the most."

"You're a reverse snob."

"And you can't see how money is bad for you. Maybe it's okay for other people—but not for you. Not for us."

"And where did you come up with that idea?"

"You don't have to look any further than your own hands."

Jewell looked at her hands. Smooth, pale skin lightly scented with Chanel No 5 Pour Le Corps. Silk tips and a perfect manicure. A square-cut diamond solitaire on her left ring finger, and three diamond anniversary bands stacked on the right ring finger.

"Where's your mother's engagement ring?" Clay asked. "You know, the one with the small diamond."

Jewell shrugged. "It didn't really go with the other jewelry," she said.

"See? Think about the kind of diamond I could afford to buy you as an engagement ring. Would it go with your other jewelry?"

Jewell bit her lip. "So what do you want to do?" she asked very quietly.

"It's time for me to go," Clay said, pulling off the pastel cashmere polo shirt she had splurged on only yesterday. "I think I'll go back to the station now."

"To live?"

"Yeah. We can't work this out as long as I'm living under your roof. I feel like a kept man. And someday, you'd think of me that way, too."

Jewell felt as if she had been punched in the stomach.

"I thought we loved each other," she said.

"We do. But not enough to survive this." He gestured around the plushly feminine bedroom. "Not enough to survive this."

He packed up quietly, putting a few jeans and work shirts into a duffel bag, careful to leave the tuxedo, the Armani suits, the alligator belt and matching tasseled loafers. Jewell stared at him without speaking.

As he finished with his packing, she got up and walked stiffly to the writing table. She pulled her checkbook from the middle drawer.

"This should pay off your mother's mortgage and also help with buying the gas station," she said woodenly.

"I don't want your money," Clay said. "I've just got done telling you that."

"We had a deal," Jewell said, recovering a little of her balance. "Take the money. Think of your mother if you don't want to think of yourself. This . . . part is purely a business transaction."

"Purely a business transaction?" Clay said, eyes narrowing.

"Yes," Jewell said, swallowing hard. "I'll be delighted to know that your mother has some security for her senior years."

She held the check out to him without looking at him. He took it from her. The small blue piece of paper fluttered and then was folded crisply into a square—it disappeared into his shirt pocket. That was their relationship: reduced, folded up, shoved into a pocket. It was money, which was the thing that had destroyed them from the start.

But maybe it wasn't just money. Maybe it was everything that went with money. Class. Education. Refinement. And a festering weakness that came with unearned wealth.

"You know what, Jewell? I'm glad to leave. Since I've moved in here, I can't find a decent place to sit. You're always telling me that this chair's upholstery cost too much per yard or that chair was the last remaining one of a set built in the seventeenth century."

"That's because your jeans are so dirty."

"That's because I work. I do work. Honest work."

"You could clean up before you come home. Besides, you don't need to work."

"A man needs to work."

"You're being sexist."

"No, I'm not. I think a woman needs to work, too. You're the finest living example of that fact. When you work, you're a warm, kindhearted, funny, beautiful woman. When you don't work, you're the most prissy, stuck-up woman I've ever met."

Jewell felt stung to her very core. But rather than cry, as she would have liked, she pursed her lips together very tightly and held her tongue.

"And let me tell you something else, Princess. The next time you want a little walk on the wild side, pick somebody without a heart, because..." His voice cracked, and Jewell looked up at him, her eyes softening for just a moment. She was ready to throw it all away to have the chance to hold him one more time. But his eyes narrowed to two hard, dark spots, and Jewell averted her own eyes.

"Because you've broken mine," Clay finished in a venomous whisper, and strode away before she could beg him to stay.

When he left, she surprised herself by not crying. Even when she heard Samson and Delilah yapping as he corralled them into the truck. She was going to miss the dogs, even if they had ripped apart her bedroom slippers and mistook a ten-pound roast for a dinner party as their own. She held her breath until the sounds of the truck pulling out from the courtyard had died away.

He was gone.

But she was beyond tears—somehow cold to the loss of love. She couldn't cry because her emotions were too complicated, too contradictory. There wasn't pure sadness over his leaving. There wasn't pure grief over his hurled insults. There wasn't pure anger over his abandonment.

Instead, she felt at war within herself. A war between the desire to give everything for love and the good sense to know that she could throw everything away for him and there would still be no guarantee that they would be happy.

Jewell sat at her writing table for a very long time, until at long last she realized that he was absolutely right to leave. Their love could not last because someday, perhaps someday very soon, she would look across the dinner table at him, or perhaps across the linen sheets, and she would say to herself, *I made him what he is.*

And there was nothing that would destroy Clay and destroy her love for him more completely than for either of them to believe that.

Doomed. There was no way around the conclusion that they were doomed, that they had never had a chance.

And that's when the tears came to her, wrenched from the very center of her being.

TWENTY MINUTES LATER, with a light dusting of ivory powder on her cheeks and a fresh coat of mascara, Jewell descended the wide, velvet-runnered staircase to the front hallway. Her guests had congregated in the living room, where Mia was serving mint juleps, pouring flutes of champagne and passing a tray of canapés.

Jewell kept a tight smile plastered to her face as she expertly deflected questions about Clay. She had grown up with a full arsenal of polite phrases and

Emily Post-approved comments. Within minutes and without great emotion, the entire guest list had come to understand that they had misunderstood—Clay was just a passing fancy.

And her fancy had passed on to other things.

By the time Jewell led her guests to the conservatory, where three tables had been set, the party had absorbed this information and had gone off to other topics of consideration. The first course was goat cheese and arugula salad with roasted walnuts, and the admiration for the voluptuous centerpiece was loud. Soon the topic of conversation was florists—who was good, who lacked a certain creativity, who charged far too much for his or her services.

As the plates were cleared away by anonymous young men who had been hired by Mia for the occasion, a second course of baked chicken with a balsamic rice pilaf was brought out. After thanking her guests for their compliments, Jewell slipped out of the conservatory and headed for the empty breakfast room.

She stood with her forehead pressed to the pane of the French doors leading to the garden. She stared out onto the garden and, as she watched the gardener supervise the clearing of some underbrush, she realized she was simply seeing a scene from her younger days. She could imagine Clay, work shirt clinging to his chest with sweat, his skin brown as café au lait, his burnished calluses throbbing with pain.

Had she really been so cossetted and protected that he had worked every day for her family and she had never noticed?

She knew the answer was yes. She had never noticed the workers who kept the gardens lush and beautiful, who manicured the lawns, who cleaned the house and repaired the roof every time a major storm passed through. She had barely ever spoken to Mia, who had devoted nearly every day of her life to caring for Jewell's every need.

And now there was something very painful about seeing the gardener at work with his helpers. She almost called out to Mia to tell them to go home, come back tomorrow, don't torture her today with their presence. But she stopped herself as she realized how dictatorial she would sound, how she was creating her own prison, a prison of wealth and privilege where she would cage herself from feeling the pain of Clay's leaving.

"You have given, as usual, a wonderful luncheon," a voice interrupted.

She turned around to see Rev. Copland, who, rather than hesitating to intrude, plopped down on the cushions of a wicker chair.

"But you're not feeling well?" he asked.

She took a deep breath and nearly answered him with a pat, hostesslike answer. One designed to deflect and redirect conversation to weather, upcoming social events, the latest quirky news from southern California or how his work at the church was going.

Instead, she simply sat down next to him.

"It's impossible," she said. "It's impossible for me to be involved with Clay, but it hurts so much. I've never been in love before. But it can't work out, you know."

"I know," Rev. Copland said.

"Are you going to tell me something comforting about how I'll find someone else?" Jewell asked, fighting her tears.

"No, because I have no way of knowing whether that would be the truth or not. Perhaps there is nobody else like Clay. Perhaps there are other men whom you would love better. Perhaps there aren't. All I know is that you are a seeker, and you will seek and find something to satisfy the spiritual hunger inside you."

"A seeker?"

"Oh, yes, it's the only way I can find of explaining how you've moved through your life. Look at how you have studied everything from cooking to social work to art to literature."

"I moved on. I started cooking school because I thought I wanted to have my own restaurant, and then social work because I realized how much pain there was in the world and then art because I wanted to express myself, but then I realized literature was... I don't know."

"Did you move on because you were bored?"

"Oh, no," Jewell protested. "I moved on each time because..." She thought carefully, looking at herself and her history and not liking what she saw.

"I moved on because each time I reached a point where I would have to sacrifice something, have to make a commitment to reach the next level. Like with cooking, I'd have to have actually started work on opening the restaurant and it... scared me. And with social work, I nearly got a master's, but I couldn't finish my thesis."

"And about Clay?"

"Oh, Reverend, that's a completely different situation," Jewell said. "He's the one leaving me. Everything was perfect, everything was great—I would have been happy to make a commitment to him. He's the one who wanted out."

"Is that so?" Rev. Copland said archly.

Jewell stared out the window at the rolling fields that had belonged to the Whittington family for so long.

"Reverend, what would you do with Pontchartreaux if it were yours."

"If it were truly mine? I would make it a refuge for women and children to make the transition from hard times to self-sufficiency. A helping hand that wouldn't require ten forms in triplicate or face budget cuts at every election or make a perfectly hardy adult dependent and degraded and convinced that she is never again going to hold a decent job."

Jewell smiled. "Sounds very nice."

"Yes, but Pontchartreaux is yours, Jewell, to do with what you want. You can do anything—turn it into a shelter, make it an artists' colony, live here in solitude, raise a family in it, make it into a museum, sell it to a developer to divide it into tract homes. You have a hundred choices, Jewell, and only the one that makes you happy is right."

And with that, the reverend discreetly turned and greeted several guests who, their luncheons finished, had come in search of their hostess. The reverend shepherded these from the sun room, explaining that Jewell was "indisposed."

Long after the last goodbyes and final *such a nice brunch*es were said, long after the last car glided out of the courtyard, long after the reverend stood at the doorway and said a farewell that required no response, Jewell stared out the window.

She was still there when the afternoon's rain came up from the delta, and when she saw her face in the window, she couldn't tell if there were tears or raindrops falling on her reflected face.

## Chapter Twelve

"Grand opening," Al said. "The sign says Grand Opening. You think I oughta take you over there for a bite to eat?"

A grumbling from under the hood of a '67 Mustang was his response.

"Clay, you've got a restaurant opening up next door to you," Al said. "Don't you want to check it out?"

Clay looked up and muttered something darkly to his brother. Then he returned to work. Al sat down on the gas-pump island's curb.

"This has been going on too long," he said. "You don't come by as much as you used to. You don't eat. You look mad all the time...."

"That's because I am. I'm mad. And I don't eat because I don't want to eat. And I don't want anybody's company."

"Well, yeah, okay," Al said, fumbling with his glasses. "Hell, Clay, you got me off my train of thought. I'm supposed to point out something to you that you don't already know. This talk is supposed to be a revelation to you."

"Give it a whirl."

"I was going to point out that you're miserable."

"Yeah, I know."

"And that you're not the same."

"I know that."

"That if you act like this for too much longer, people'll start to talk."

"I suspect they already are."

Clay flipped the lid of the Mustang and reached for a paper towel to wipe his grease-stained hands.

"All right, I'll tell you something I'm sure you don't already know," Al said to his back as Clay headed for the door to the office. "You're in love."

Clay stopped.

He turned around and faced his younger brother.

"You're wrong, buddy. Being in love with her would mean that I thought she was wonderful. And I don't. She's spoiled, demanding, bossy, snobbish and she has absolutely no common sense. And she doesn't understand a thing about me or my needs. And she doesn't understand the kind of woman she'll become if she keeps herself cooped up in her castle."

Having made that clear, Clay walked away from Al.

Al took off his glasses to wipe some dust particles away and then put them back on. He trotted after his brother into the office. Clay was working at the cash register, calculating charges for the Mustang.

"You really had me going," Al said, leaning on the counter. "I really believed you. But you forgot to mention that she's gorgeous."

Clay shrugged without looking up from his totaling of the Mustang's cured ills.

"Yeah, I guess she is."

"And she's a great dancer."

Clay nodded. "She is."

"And when she wants to, she's a great listener, got a great personality, is nice to everyone and works real hard."

"So what?"

"So you love her."

Clay shook his head, wrote "Void" in bold letters across the Mustang's invoice and turned it so that Al could read it.

"It doesn't matter whether I love her," Clay said flatly. "She's gone. We broke up. She's not coming back."

"And you can't go back to her?"

"Won't do any good. I don't have anything to offer her."

"You own your own business. Ma's house is paid for, so you don't owe money to anybody. All of us kids are raised and self-sufficient. What more do you need to offer a girl?"

Without meaning to, Clay's hand reached into his pocket to feel—for the thousandth time—the diamond solitaire ring.

Less than a carat.

Bought for his mother by his dad.

He had wanted to give it to Jewell.

Had kept it in the pocket of whatever elegant shirt she had asked him to wear, waiting for the right moment.

But that moment had never come.

"I got one major liability," Clay explained. "One sinkhole down which all my financial resources are going."

"What's that?"

"Your car," Clay said, pointing to the Mustang's charge sheet. "You know, if you don't take care of it, it's going to spend more time in my garage than it is in yours."

"But it doesn't matter if I don't take care of it. I've got a brother who will."

Clay ripped the sheet from the pad and handed it to Al.

Al looked at the sheet, with the word "Void" scrawled across the list of repairs made to his car.

"How are you ever going to make a profit if you do all your friends and family for free?" Al asked. "I heard you did Mrs. McGillivray's transmission for no charge last week."

"She's living on a fixed income. I would feel like a jerk charging her."

"And you're doing all my work for free, too."

"You're my kid brother. But I am charging you. Sort of."

"You are?"

"Yeah, dinner. And considering I've just rebuilt your engine, I think you're getting off cheap."

Al smiled. "Come on, I know just the place. It just opened. You'll love it."

AT THREE O'CLOCK, the Pretty Good Café was empty. Al and Clay took two places at the counter.

"Looks like whoever reopened the place did a good job," Clay mused.

Cheery white lace curtains and blue gingham valances at the windows. Blue gingham tablecloths, white cotton napkins, and the floors had been scrubbed and bleached down to the pale oak. A waitress put two glasses of water in front of the men and asked them what they'd be having.

Clay opened the menu—a new one, without the familiar grease stains and misspelled words—and chose the chicken-fried-steak special. Al did the same. While they waited for their meal, they talked about the family and some friends in common.

"Al, you look like you're hiding something from me," Clay commented. "What are you all smiles about?"

"Oh, nothing."

"Great. My life is in shambles, and my brother is giggling like an eighth grader."

Just then the waitress put their orders in front of them. The chipped white crockery of the Pretty Good Café had been updated with Blue Willow china. Clay closed his eyes as he smelled the fragrant spices.

As he opened his eyes, he noticed something unusual on his plate. "What's this?"

"It's a rosette," the waitress said. "Made out of a cherry tomato. You should order the key lime pie for dessert, each piece has got a candied violet on it. And you can eat them, too. I've had to tell so many customers. It's okay, they're not poisonous. And you should see the French fries. They're cut kinda different. It's called juli-end."

Clay looked around the café, as if seeing it for the first time. Sure, he had noticed it was better looking than before. But it was the little touches that suddenly seemed to reach out and grab him. The coffeepot in the waitress's hand was sterling. The salt at each table was in cut crystal. The lithographs over the booths were original nineteenth century—he recognized them.

And there was a Renoir woodcut over the cash register.

He recognized it from his one attempt at a life of crime.

"Excuse me," he said to Al.

He jumped over the counter and marched into the kitchen.

Jewell, in jeans and a faded gray T-shirt, stood at the stove, stirring a fragrant vanilla sauce. She turned around, showing off her pixie-ish haircut and her impish smile.

"Hi! I guess we're going to be neighbors," she said brightly.

"What now?" Clay groaned.

"Aren't you happy to see me?"

"Not really," Clay said sourly. "Is having a restaurant your life mission of the week?"

She remained unexpectedly upbeat. "No, Clay, it's my life."

"For how long?"

"Forever."

"Yeah, sure."

"No, really."

"At the end of the day, do you go home and Mia makes you a glass of champagne for you to drink on the veranda?"

Jewell shook her head. "Pontchartreaux isn't mine any longer."

Clay's eyes narrowed. "What do you mean?"

"The Reverend Copland runs a shelter in it. With all the room, it can house thirty women with their children. I'm on the board that oversees the shelter, but I don't live there anymore. They don't have room for me.''

"What about your studies?''

"I've learned more in the past month with you than I did in the past decade at school.''

"What about all your money?''

"I had to give something to the reverend to get the shelter started,'' she said. "Although I used some of it to spruce up this café a little. And four thousand to the Duncans. Remember that couple with the triplets?''

"Yeah, I remember. You gave away all of it, gone?'' Clay asked, stunned.

"All of it,'' Jewell confirmed. "Gone. Everything's either in this café or in the shelter. I don't even have a place to stay yet.''

"Let me see your hands.''

Jewell held out her hands. Her nails were unpolished and short but neatly filed. And her skin was slightly red and puckered from washing the lunch-crowd dishes.

Her mother's diamond was her only adornment.

Clay reached into his pocket and pulled out his own family ring. He slipped it onto her ring finger, up against her mother's ring.

"Look at that, they're the same ring,'' Clay said.

"Oh, I bet my parents and yours bought them at the same store,'' Jewell said. "Clay, does this mean you want to...?''

"Yeah, it does. It means I want to spend the rest of my life with you. Especially if we're going to be neighbors.''

He swept her up in his arms, carrying her out to the dining room. Past his grinning brother and the astonished waitress.

"Check the vanilla sauce, don't let it burn!" Jewell shouted as the bells on the door jingled in their wake.

Clay strode across the empty street.

"What made you do it?" he asked, nuzzling her ear in a deliciously torturous portent of pleasures to come.

"Because I didn't want to grow up to be a bitter, lonely and selfish woman," Jewell said. "And because I love you."

"Oh, God, Jewell, I love you, too," he said.

He put her down at the door to the office, long enough to reach inside and flip the Open sign to Sorry We're Closed. Then he led her up the fire escape to the apartment. Samson and Delilah roused themselves from the bed and stared at their humans in astonishment.

"Move it, Samson. Get out of here, Delilah," Clay ordered good-naturedly. "We're home. We're really home."

And then he flung himself down on the bed, pulling her down on top of him.

"If we're engaged now, we'd better head for the courthouse," Jewell teased. "I thought you were in favor of short engagements."

"Why don't we compromise?" Clay suggested huskily. "An eighteen-hour engagement—meet you at the courthouse at nine tomorrow morning."

"Long white dress? Flowers flown in from Holland? Champagne and caviar?"

Clay shook his head. "Jeans. Flowers from my ma's garden. And breakfast at Al's. No, you make the breakfast. Getting married'll be nice—I'll only have to walk across the street for a decent meal.''

He smothered her giggles with his own hard, proud mouth.

Their first kiss of a new life tasted sweet and fresh and full of promise. And as he peeled the T-shirt from her shoulders and shuddered in pleasure at the sight of her naked flesh, he squeezed his eyes shut for a brief prayer of thanksgiving. He was the luckiest man in the world; he had everything kings and emperors had ever lusted for, because this knight at last had his princess.

# HARLEQUIN®
# AMERICAN ◆ ROMANCE®
### ®

## *Maybe This Time...*

Maybe this time...they'll get what they really wanted all those years ago. Whether it's the man who got away, a baby, or a new lease on life, these four women will get a second chance at a once-in-a-lifetime opportunity!

Four top-selling authors have come together to make you believe that in the world of American Romance anything is possible:

**#642 ONE HUSBAND TOO MANY**
Jacqueline Diamond
August

**#646 WHEN A MAN LOVES A WOMAN**
Bonnie K. Winn
September

**#650 HEAVEN CAN WAIT**
Emily Dalton
October

**#654 THE COMEBACK MOM**
Muriel Jensen
November

Look us up on-line at: http://www.romance.net

MTTG

**UNLOCK THE DOOR TO GREAT ROMANCE
AT BRIDE'S BAY RESORT**

Join Harlequin's new across-the-lines series, set
in an exclusive hotel on an island off the coast of
South Carolina.

Seven of your favorite authors will bring you exciting stories
about fascinating heroes and heroines discovering love at
Bride's Bay Resort.

Look for these fabulous stories coming to a store near you
beginning in January 1996.

**Harlequin American Romance #613** in January
*Matchmaking Baby* by Cathy Gillen Thacker

**Harlequin Presents #1794** in February
*Indiscretions* by Robyn Donald

**Harlequin Intrigue #362** in March
*Love and Lies* by Dawn Stewardson

**Harlequin Romance #3404** in April
*Make Believe Engagement* by Day Leclaire

**Harlequin Temptation #588** in May
*Stranger in the Night* by Roseanne Williams

**Harlequin Superromance #695** in June
*Married to a Stranger* by Connie Bennett

**Harlequin Historicals #324** in July
*Dulcie's Gift* by Ruth Langan

Visit Bride's Bay Resort each month wherever
Harlequin books are sold.

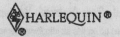

**Sabrina**     **It Happened One Night**
**Working Girl**     **Pretty Woman**
**While You Were Sleeping**

If you adore romantic comedies then have we got the books for you!

Beginning in **August 1996** head to your favorite retail outlet for
**LOVE & LAUGHTER™,**
a brand-new series with two books every month capturing the lighter side of love.

You'll enjoy humorous love stories by favorite authors and brand-new writers, including JoAnn Ross, Lori Copeland, Jennifer Crusie, Kasey Michaels, and many more!

As an added bonus—with the retail purchase, of two new Love & Laughter books you can receive a **free** copy of our fabulous Love and Laughter collector's edition.

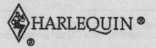

**LOVE & LAUGHTER™**—a natural combination...always romantic...always entertaining

**HARLEQUIN**®